Neither Good nor Evil

S.M Robinson

The Seaquel Publishing—Lynchburg, VA
ISBN: 979-8-9854001-0-6
Title: *Neither Good nor Evil*
Author: S.M Robinson
Digital distribution | 2021
Paperback | 2021

There are people in the world who are willing to make the ultimate sacrifice for the ones they love in a blink of an eye. Not knowing what, who and why they are sacrificing for. They never stop to think if they would just put the work in to do the right thing, just maybe the sacrificial lamb isn't what they really needed to bargain with.

Table of Contents

Chapter 1
Unexplained

It was the evening of the last day of school and Arielle could hear her siblings, Adriel and Adeena, playing with their friends, Charles and Sasha in the front of the yard. Her father, Edward, went to get pizza to celebrate everyone graduating to the next grade and she had never been prouder of herself as she was going to first grade. Her mother, Daniela, had called her to come and get cleaned up as she knew he would be returning soon. Once Arielle reached the door, she could hear her father turning into the driveway. She smiled and headed into the house. As she went to wash her hands, there was a scream.

Arielle came running out of the house to see what the fuss was about. At the end of the driveway, Arielle could see her sister Adeena was with her friend Sasha. Her brother Adriel and his friend Charles were at the front gate by Charles' bike. As Arielle and her mother approached, she saw the rest of them looking at something on the ground. Adeena was holding Sasha while she was crying. Arielle figured Sasha was the one that screamed since she was crying. Her father walked back to Arielle and her mother telling them to stop.

Arielle pushed past her father and ran towards her brother as he was standing over top of it. He grabbed her. Arielle then saw that it was her cat, Miles. Her father picked her up as she heard loud whaling, but didn't know where it was coming from. She looked around while everyone was staring back at her. She then turned her head when saw something out of the corner of her eye. There was a dark shadowy figure off into the distance under the lamppost. She struggled to see what it was. Her eyes became heavy and it suddenly was hard to see after a while and she fainted.

"What happened?" said Daniela.

"I didn't see him, I swear. I thought I hit a pothole in our driveway," said Marcus.

"No, I mean what happened with Arielle? I never heard her scream like that before, and she passed out," said Daniela.

Marcus was perplexed as he rubbed his forehead and said, "I've never seen anyone react like that before. She is different, but maybe we should give her some time to take it in."

Daniela was frustrated.

She said, "You have to fix this, and fix the driveway before anything else happens."

Arielle woke up in a good mood, but hungry. She had forgotten all about what happened a few hours ago. She went to the bathroom and washed her hands. She could see Mile's litter box and she realized what had just happened moments ago. Tears flowed from her eyes as images poured into her mind. She stood at the sink while the water was running.

Adriel walked pass the bathroom singing and looked over at her. At first, he didn't notice, he stopped and walked back to her slowly. He turned the water off, sat on the toilet, and held her tightly. She fell into his arms and let herself go. They sat there for a while and when she felt like she was done, she walked away.

Adeena was outside the door standing, waiting for them to come out. When Adriel came out, Adeena said, "You never did that for me."

"We're like twins Adeena. We have each other's back. You don't need it," he said with a grin and patted her on the shoulder.

Adeena was always jealous of Adriel and Arielle's relationship. They are eleven months apart. People had mistaken them to be twins all the time. He loves being his sister's twin, but she hates that he gets all the attention.

Adeena went to her room and sat on her bed. She pondered over what she has just seen. She could never understand why her brother doesn't love her as much as he loves Arielle. She thinks about what she could do to make him give her that type of affection. She starts looking around her room. The only thing she has is her goldfish, Jasper. How can she make him believe that her heart is broken? Arielle loved Miles, the cat that died their dog, and Peppa the dog dearly. Adeena knows that it will take some time to put this plan together.

While Adeena was plotting for her brother's affection, Arielle is heading into the kitchen to get something to eat. She didn't realize it was late. Daniela warmed up the food and set it on the table. She knew by hearing her crying in the bathroom with Adriel that she would be coming down soon to eat. Arielle knew that her brother would not tell their mother a word about what happened in the bathroom, so she didn't have to worry about her mother asking any questions. Arielle wiped her face and sat down.

Her mother asked, "Do you want something to drink? Water or milk?"

Arielle signed water as she never actually has spoken a word. Her words come out as gibberish, but Sunshine, her imaginary friend, seems to understand her perfectly.

Arielle ate her food and went back to her room. Daniela was worried about Arielle not being able to express herself about what happened. She spends time with her imaginary friend, and she bonded with Adriel more than anyone else.

Arielle trusted Adriel. Adriel doesn't judge her, and he understands her. Daniela tries not to judge her, but it was very hard not to since she has an imaginary friend. She was starting to think that she was going to need help soon to make it in school if she didn't stop pretending.

Arielle called for Sunshine to come and talk to her, but Sunshine didn't answer her. She was upset and began to cry. Adriel was heading up the stairs and sensed something was wrong. He came to her room to check on her before he went to his room for the night. He saw she had paper and pencil out, but he knew she didn't know how to write.

"Is there something you want me to write for Sunshine tonight," he asked?

She nodded her head, but before she started to sign, she saw Adriel begin writing what she was thinking.

He wrote, "If I am asleep when you come tonight, please wake me up. Something bad happened today."

He didn't realize what had happened at that moment, but he kissed her on the forehead and told her it would be okay. Arielle wanted to tell him what happened and she tried to stop him as he walked out the room by putting her hand up to reach for him. As he left, Peppa trotted into the room and jumped on the bed

Arielle fell asleep crying thinking about Miles. Her dreams were all over the place. As the sun rose, she had a nightmare. Sweat was pouring down her face and she woke up with a jolt. Her eyes filled with tears. She looked around her room and Peppa was off the bed over by her dresser growling at the door. She waved her hand for Peppa to come back, but Peppa growled one more time before she ran over to her. Arielle looked at the door and didn't see anything. She realized that her wrist was hurting. As she grabbed it, Peppa licked her face and then her wrist. She sat on her bed trying to figure out why her wrist was hurting and why Peppa was growling at the door.

Later that morning, Adriel came down to eat breakfast listening to his music and singing. He saw Arielle and rubbed her head. His mother gave him his plate. She asked, "Where is Adeena?"

He replied, "She hasn't come out of her room yet."

Their mother yelled upstairs for her. No answer. She yelled again. No answer. She asked their father to get her.

He had been sitting in the living room drinking coffee reading the morning paper.

He said, "It's summertime for the kids, why can't she sleep in for a little while longer."

She replied, "I have things that need to be done, as well as you do. It may be Saturday, unfortunately, getting to town and back takes time and she knows that."

Marcus reluctantly went upstairs, knocked on her door, announced himself, then opened it. Adeena was in the mirror putting make-up on her face and her hair was cut.

He yelled out, "What in Sam Hell is going on here? You go to that bathroom and clean that off your face right now young lady. Daniela, where did she get this make-up from?"

Daniela ran up the stairs. Daniela was in shock at what she saw.

Adeena's reaction was very calm with no remorse. She said, "It's moms, she gave it to me."

Daniela denied the entire thing while Marcus scolded her.

Adriel had put earbuds in Arielle's ears so she could only hear the music and he smiled at her.

Once Daniela and Marcus came downstairs they went outside to discuss what just happened. Arielle and Adriel finished their food, and they went to get dressed for the day.

Later, Adeena came downstairs and was dressed in black ripped shorts with fishnet stockings, black boots, ripped shirt with black fingernail polish.

Arielle was confused, but thinks, "Cool." She smiled at Adeena and gave her a thumbs up.

Adeena told her, "Whatever little twerp," and went to get in the vehicle.

Adriel came out of the house and he had two sets of headphones in his hands. He got in the vehicle and leaned back to get Arielle's attention.

He said, "I got something for you."

He had an extra iPod with headphones.

With a smile, he said, "I made a playlist for you. Since this is a long ride you may want to hear music that you like instead of the radio."

Arielle took it with a huge smile on her face and looked it over trying to figure out how to use it.

Adeena looked at him with pure hate. She folded her arms and looked out the window, holding back tears as he explained everything to Arielle. The more he was talking the more she got infuriated. Adriel couldn't see that it bothered Adeena.

Meanwhile, Marcus and Daniela finished discussing the agenda. Neither one of them had seen what Adeena was wearing. Marcus reached for Daniela and pulled her towards him. She resisted as she was still angry from him yelling at her earlier.

He told her. "I should've known she was lying sweetheart. I'm sorry. I should've asked you first before assuming the worst. Can you please forgive me?"

She said, "Darling it's not that you assumed, it's the fact that you yelled at me in front of the kids. This is something that we promised we would never do. I love you with all my heart. I fought hard to be a good person and raise the kids without violence in the home, but you are making the first step of the problem. What will be next? So, if you are sorry, prove it to me."

As Daniela walks away, Marcus yells out, "I am not your father!"

She replies, "You are far from him," and she blows him a kiss and waves goodbye.

They begin heading down the road while Adriel and Arielle were listening to their music and Daniela was playing the radio, Adeena shows her agitation.

Adeena says, "Since they have their music can you at least change the station to something I would want to listen to?"

Daniela looked back in the rear-view mirror and said, "You know the rules, my car, my music."

Adeena gives her a glare of hatred and replies, "How come I don't have anything to listen to and they do?"

As Daniela looks at her, she notices her clothes. She tried not to respond in anger or react in any way that would spark an outburst from Adeena.

She thinks to herself, "No ma'am. This child is testing me."

Daniela said, "I didn't give Arielle anything, Adriel did, so sorry. I can't help you with that. When you get to Grandma Pearl's, ask her for one for your birthday next year or Christmas. She was the one that gave one to him for his birthday. Then last year Grandpa gave him one for Christmas. I think your mind is in the wrong place right now and."

"Everyone is in the wrong place and it's not fair, this is bullshit!" Adeena belted out.

"Adeena! Watch your tongue," Daniela exclaimed. "I will not have you using that language. I suggest you calm yourself down before you get in a lot of trouble, young lady. Now sit back and be quiet for the rest of the ride before we have any further issues."

Adriel heard the whole conversation but didn't react. He was very shocked at how Adeena talked to their mother. She never used to be like that. He never once heard her use a curse word before. Was it because the cat died or was it because he was hugging their baby sister in the bathroom? They have gone through worse things than that. People have tried to beat her up before and she has pounded on them like they were a sack of potatoes. He thought it was weird that she put the make-up on because she never liked seeing make-up on females. She would call it a mask covering up their inner beauty. Adriel looked in the side view mirror, watching the road behind them. A small glimpse showed his little sister bobbing her head to the playlist he selected for her. He turned up his music and it wiped out the conversation in his head.

They arrived in town, and they ran into their neighbors Catherine and Jordan Peters at the hardware store.

Catherine said to her husband, "Jordan, there's Daniela, I am going to go over and chat with her."

Jordan waved his hand at her shoving her off as he was talking to the sales clerk about seeds to plant his vegetable garden. They were a retired couple, but they loved hanging out with Daniela and Marcus Gibson when they could. The Peter's met the Gibson's when they first moved to town and Daniela was pregnant with Adriel. They were the ones that helped pick out Adriel's name as their son's name was Adrienne. He passed away when he was twelve riding his bike on the road.

Catherine walked up to Daniela and hugged her. Daniela said, "I see Jordan is still a mister busy body, looking at the seeds. Is he trying to do a vegetable garden this time?"

"Unfortunately, yes. He thought that if we grew our own stuff, we wouldn't have to come out here that often. You know as well as I do, I will be here as often as I can to get away from that old coot," she said with a laugh. "What are you guys up to today," Catherine asked.

Daniela pulled Catherine away while the kids were wandering around the store to make sure they didn't hear her talking to her.

She said, "Well unfortunately we had an accident at the house with Miles. I made an excuse to come to town. Marcus and I decided to purchase another cat for Arielle since she was so attached to him. I haven't told Arielle yet. I figure we stop here first before we do that so we don't open up any wounds yet."

Catherine looked back at Arielle with a somber face and said, "Poor baby, she is so attached to the animals, well you're doing the right thing sweetheart. You're a good mother if there ever is one. You keep doing what you're doing. I do have to ask, what's going on with Deena honey? Did someone take her to the barn and beat her with a broomstick?"

Daniela shakes her head in shame, "I think she cracked her skull overnight or fell out of the bed. She pulled this out of nowhere. When I say I have no idea what is going on with her, I mean it. She told Marcus I gave her make-up to put on, she put those awful clothes on and then snapped at me in the car on the way here like some banshee in the night. I wanted to pull the car over and give her a one-two like my mama used to."

Catherine takes Daniela by the arm intensely and says, "Pay attention to what is going on. If you're not going to discipline her, then get her some professional help sweetheart."

Daniela thought hard about what she said for a few seconds and then shook it off.

She replied, "Well I think it's just a phase, she will be fine. She must be going through a pre-teen phase. She will be okay."

Catherine decided to change the subject, "Where are y'all headed to next after here?"

Daniela knew that Catherine tended to forget things so she replied, "We are going to pick out the cat for Arielle then we are headed over to go see my mother. After that, get groceries and go back home."

Oh, nice! Do you think I can tag along? I think Jordan will be here for a while anyway. We have to go to the grocery store later this evening too and I don't want to be talking to myself. As you know, he doesn't listen to the words I am saying anyway," she chuckles.

Daniela agreed and Catherine walked over and told Jordan that she would be with them. He threw his hand up again and she told him she would call him later.

They arrived at the shelter. Arielle was so excited that she ran directly to the cat section with Adriel's hand in hers.

Catherine pulls Adeena aside and tells her, "You're with me."

Adeena sighed.

Daniela went to the salesman to talk about prices for the kittens. Arielle looked at every kennel. Each kennel had three kittens in them and there were over six kennels and none of the kittens looked like Miles. She was starting to get upset.

Adriel noticed and pulled her aside and said, "I know you're looking for a kitten that looks like Miles, but you will never find another kitten just like him. You are going to have to find one that speaks to you."

Arielle was confused. She didn't know what that meant.

Adriel saw the look on her face and said, "Walk slowly down this hallway and if somehow you stop, turn to that kennel. I want you to pick out the kitten you think or feel is best for you."

Arielle started walking down the long hallway, she looked back at Adriel.

He said, "No, turn around and keep walking slowly until you get an urge to stop."

She looked back at him to confirm what he said. She hesitantly kept walking and oddly a shadowy figure was at the end of the hallway. All she could see were these crystal blue eyes. It made her stop in mid-step. She thought this was what her brother meant, but she wasn't sure. When she turned to look at the kittens and turned back to see the shadow, it was gone. This time she wasn't scared of it. She took the shadow as a sign that one of the kittens in there was the one she was supposed to pick. She went to the kennel and one of the kittens walked up to the window and licked it. Arielle smiled and thought to herself this is the one. She turned and pointed with a huge smile on her face.

Chapter 2
Disappeared

"It's time for you to die, you useless piece of crap," Adeena said as she went into the bathroom to flush Jasper down the toilet.

Dexter, the new kitten, came in and rubbed on her leg.

She said, "Get away from me you furball. Can't you see I'm busy?"

She stopped and thought for a second. Adeena leaned down into the toilet and took the fish out. She then turned to Dexter and tried to feed it to him. Dexter turned his face from her hand.

Adeena said, "No Dexter eat."

Dexter looks back at her and smacks Jasper out of her hand onto the floor. She got frustrated and picked Jasper up. The fish is now gasping for air and she tried again. Jasper finally died in her hand. Adeena pushed Jasper to Dexter's mouth again. Dexter bites down on it.

She said, "Good Dexter," with a smile.

She picked him up, brought him into her room, and put him on her dresser by the bowl. She screamed.

Her mother came in asking, "What's wrong?"

"Dexter ate Jasper! I came in from the bathroom and saw this" Adeena exclaimed. She tried to sound convincing, but there were no tears.

Her mother looked at her, then looked at the bowl then back at Dexter. He saw there was no water on the dresser. Just Dexter still chewing on something and a half-empty fishbowl. She then remembered the conversation she had with Catherine at the hardware store and she decided to play along with Adeena.

"Adeena, I will figure something out for you, I am so sorry that the cat did this. Is there anything you need me to do?"

Adeena was very shocked that her mother believed her and she forgot she was supposed to be upset about her fish.

She responded with a smile, "Yes, get rid of the cat immediately."

Daniela took him out without saying a word.

Adeena was so excited that she had full control. She never thought she could do that. She couldn't wait to tell her brother. Then she realized that she couldn't tell him because he wasn't talking to her. He wasn't the one that came to her rescue, it was her mother. Her excitement came to a halt. She stormed to his room and opened the door. He wasn't there. She went to her sister's room. She was in there talking to her imaginary friend and Adriel wasn't there. She got angrier as she noticed that she couldn't find him. How could he leave without telling her? This has never happened before. So, she decided to go find Charles and see if they were hanging out.

Adriel and Charles were by the creek skipping rocks and making jokes about things that had happened at school. Adriel was trying not to think about home or anything that reminded him of it when Charles brought up the dead cat.

"Hey Ads, remember when your dad killed your cat? That was something right," he said with a snicker.

Adriel didn't know what to say. He was taken off guard by the statement.

He replied, "Um, yeah."

Charles said, "Hey, I have a slingshot my dad gave me, I have been practicing on some cans at the house, do you want to try it out?"

Adriel looked around and said, "We don't have any cans to shoot at out here. Maybe some other time at your house."

"Dude we can shoot some birds or squirrels," as Charles laughs. He continues, "Target practice is what I need anyway. Come on, it's fun."

Adriel replies without showing how disgusted he was, "You need the practice, not me, buddy, go ahead."

Adriel was wondering why everyone was changing around him all of a sudden. First his sister and now his best friend?

Charles started pulling back at the band to aim at a bird and then they heard, "Don't even think about Charles."

They turned around and saw Sasha was coming from up the hill. Adriel was so relieved. He didn't want to see the poor bird killed.

Charles was frustrated.

He said, "Aw come on Sasha you totally messed my psyche."

"Well too bad Charles I'm sure Ads had enough of killing for one summer, I know I have. Whatcha doing out here other than being a jerk," Sasha said while she stumped down the hill.

Adriel walked over to her to reach out his hand to make sure she didn't fall.

He said, "Oh nothing just skipping rocks, talking about stupid stuff that happened at school this year and what we want to do this summer."

Sasha looked around and said, "Where's Deena?"

"Don't know," Adriel said with a straight face. He didn't want anyone to know that he and Adeena were having issues. He knew where she was and he didn't care.

When he said it, Adeena was several trees back listening and staying out of sight. She could tell that her brother didn't care about her anymore. She knew that he was about to turn their friends against her. She became infuriated and turned to head back home.

When Adeena returned to the house, she was in deep thought. It got interrupted as she noticed that her father was sitting on the front porch staring at her so intently walking up to the house. The lawn wasn't cut and he was drinking lemonade in the rocking chair. She squinted her eyes at him thinking that would help her figure out why he looked at her that way. Marcus wasn't the type that told you everything he was thinking and she often thought she could read his mind, but this time she was so consumed with what her brother was doing she missed the obvious.

When she got to the first step he yelled, "Stop! Turn around and head to the lawnmower."

Adeena said, "Excuse me?"

Marcus kept rocking and didn't hesitate in his response and said, "Turn your body around, get on the lawnmower, and cut the grass."

Before she could say anything, he said, "You say another word I will make you cut the Peters lawn as well for the next two months. So, I suggest you get on that lawnmower and cut the grass young lady before nightfall."

Adeena turned around and stumped over to the lawnmower.

She wanted to tell her mother what he was doing because she thought it was completely unfair being this was Adriel's job. He was down by the creek plotting to take her friends away from her. Her life was unfolding day by day and nobody cared.

As she got to the back of the house, she looked up at her sister's room and saw this dark shadow disappear from the window. While she was looking back at the shadow, she didn't notice a big limb on the ground in front of the lawnmower. She mowed right over the top of it. The lawnmower flipped over. She flew right off it. Her father came around back to see out what happened.

A few minutes later, Adriel came home and his father brought Adeena onto the back porch. She had blood running down her right leg and both her hands.

Arielle comes outside to check on her and Adeena yells at her to get away.

She said, "Don't touch me, you creepy little girl."

Arielle ran back into the house to her room.

Adriel couldn't believe what Adeena had said to her. He was disgusted and asked her, "Why are you so mean, she didn't do anything?"

Adeena said, "You didn't see what I saw, it's Sunshine's fault, I saw it. She and her creepy friend did it."

She sat there crying, while their father and Adriel were perplexed.

Daniela was at Catherine's getting advice. She received a call from Marcus telling her what just happened. He also told her what Adeena said about Sunshine.

Daniela shook her head.

She said, "Well thank you for trying to discipline her, but it backfired, unfortunately," with a laugh. She continued, "I appreciate your effort sweetie. I will be back in a few. I am glad she is okay, well physically," with a pause. "Okay, bye-bye."

Catherine was concerned and asked, "What happened?"

Daniela took a big breath and said, "She is blaming Arielle and her imaginary friend Sunshine for her running over a branch in the yard without looking."

Catherine belted out a laugh which made Daniela laugh.

This triggered Jordan to come and see what all the noise was about. They apologized to him and then chuckled quietly.

Catherine told Daniela, "Look child when I told you that you will have to discipline her, I didn't mean belts and whips. I meant to put a firm grip on her. She is going to a place she can't return from unless you get some help. You will have to get a psychiatrist to assist you. She may take her frustrations out on her siblings next. You can't take the kitten back just because she wants you to. You have to get her to understand she isn't the only kid in that house. Now she wants to discipline the baby because she has an imaginary friend, that's nonsense. I know a doctor that is on the other side of town named Dr. Pavlovsky. She works with kids and she is a friend of the family. I will call her in the morning and give her your number. Don't worry about anything. I will make sure she won't charge you."

Daniela was very worried and became bashful.

She said, "No Catherine, you don't have to do that, we can figure this out. You and Jordan have done so much for us."

Catherine took her hands and said, "Sweetheart it's my pleasure, Marcus and you have more than enough to deal with. Now go home and help him out. Makeup with your husband because you two will need each other during this time."

The next morning after breakfast, there was a scream coming from outside. Marcus ran to the front porch to see what happened.

Adeena laughed and said, "I just wanted to see who would come running this time, but it was just you."

Arielle was off in the distance playing with Peppa. Adriel was upstairs listening to his music so he didn't hear her. Daniela was cleaning the kitchen up from breakfast and wasn't trying to react to what Adeena was trying to do after the day before. As Marcus walked back in, Dexter slid by to go out the door.

He tells Adeena, "You better make sure you behave yourself."

She replies, "I was only just kidding with the stupid cat."

Marcus went into the kitchen and told Daniela that he was about to head out for work then kissed her.

She turned to kiss him back and asked him, "What do you want me to say to Dr. Pavlovsky?"

He said, "Tell her the truth, we won't get anything done if she doesn't know what is going on in these walls," as he points to the kitchen walls.

She smiled and said, "Yes dear." They kissed once more and he left.

A few hours later, there was a phone call and Adriel answered the phone. On the other end, a woman with a German accent asked to speak to Mrs. Gibson. Adriel was very perplexed. He put the phone down and went to get his mother.

Daniela answered the phone while Adriel sat in the kitchen pretending to be very quiet so he could hear what the conversation was about. His mother was acting as if she knew her. She was setting up a time to meet her with the family. He became worried and ran off to his room.

Daniela had no idea that Adriel had been listening from the other room. She walked up the stairs to go get his laundry from his room and noticed that his door was locked. She knocked on his door and received no answer. She knocked again, and no answer. She took out the master key and opened the door. He was lying on his bed with his headphones in and he sat up quickly.

She asked him, "Ads, what's wrong love?"

Adriel shook his head with no response. He turned his back to her and said, "You wouldn't understand even if I told you."

She put the basket down and closed his door just in case someone walked down the hallway so they wouldn't hear.

Daniela said, "Ads, I'm here for you, what's wrong sweetheart."

Adriel let out a big sigh, "I heard you on the phone. Are you and dad getting a divorce?

She hugged him and said, "Oh sweetheart, no. That call was for your sister. I made an appointment so that she can have a psychiatrist. They want to meet all of us first. I am so sorry for being secretive, but we just didn't want you guys to be worried."

Adriel looked up at her and said, "Is she going through that change that they talk about in school that girls go through," with a gross look on his face.

Daniela laughed and said, "Well sweetheart, when she goes through that you will know. It is way worse than this. How about you clean your face up and have some ice cream. Go get Arielle and see if she wants some too. I will get Adeena from outside and have her bring in Dexter."

"Okay," he said.

Adeena was looking for Dexter she realized that she had the worst job ever. She thought to herself, "Why do I have to go look for the rodent that ate my innocent Jasper. This isn't fair."

She looked behind the shed, up in the treehouse and back near the woods, but still no resolve. She came back to the house and said, "I can't find the little devil."

Daniela said, "Well you could've found a better way of saying that. Did you look behind the shed?"

Adeena replied, "It's not my stinking pet, and yes. I looked up in the treehouse and by the woods. Maybe the stupid thing got some sense after it ate my poor innocent Jasper and left."

Daniela snarled, "You fed Jasper to Dexter so stop the sassiness and sit down. Dexter should know his way back here by now. Hopefully, we will see him in an hour or two, if not we will go look for him."

Adeena looked over at Arielle and smirked.

Adriel saw what she did and had a bad feeling about it.

An hour went by and no Dexter. Arielle became worried. Sasha showed up to see if Adeena could come down to her house. Daniela told her that they were about to go look for Dexter and so Sasha decided to help. Adeena was livid. They all walked around the area calling for Dexter. Arielle was with her mother, while Sasha and Adeena went together. Adriel went alone looking for Dexter. As Adriel got closer to the creek, he noticed something hanging off a branch on a tree. It was covered in blood. He thought it was one of the squirrels that Charles had been shooting with his pebbles or maybe a bear had left behind. He noticed the fur on the animal was the same pattern as Dexter's. Adriel immediately felt nauseated.

On the tree there was writing, X MARKS THE SPOT. Immediately, Adriel remembered when they were all younger playing hopscotch. Adeena would get picked on every time she would toss the rock on the block that was by itself. She wasn't able to get her footing and she would fall. They would all yell out X marks the spot and laugh. They never knew how much it bothered her until she eventually quit playing the game. Later on, their mother made him apologize to her.

What made it evident that it had to be Adeena was the smile she gave Arielle and the fact that she hated Dexter. Adriel couldn't let his little sister see her cat like this. He dug a hole with one of the stones from the creek and buried the cat away from the tree. He cleaned his hands and came back to the house. He told them he couldn't find Dexter.

Adeena came around the corner and she asked if anyone could find Dexter because she had no luck.

Adriel thought to himself, "I am sure you didn't. You know exactly where he is."

Instead, he said, "No luck my way" as convincing as he could.

Daniela shook her head no.

Arielle knew it was getting dark and Dexter was going to be out there all alone.

Their mother looked down at Arielle and said, "I will talk to your father tonight and have him go to his shop tomorrow and print some flyers off for Dexter. We will search again tomorrow, okay?"

Adriel looked over at Adeena and she growled under her breath. It ate at him to know what she had done. He walked inside and they washed up for dinner while their mother cooked.

Chapter 3
The Meeting

Walking down the dusty road one early morning, Adriel was thinking about the dream he had that night. He is staring at his shoes holding his sister's hand as they are going door to door asking the neighbors if they can hang up the flyers with Dexter's picture on it. For some reason, he couldn't shake off the part of his dream where he saw his sister saying, "No Charles, stop!" She had blood all over her face while looking directly at him. He knew it was just a dream, but why was it bothering him so much?

A pull came to his arm and a little voice was in his head saying, "Do we have to go to the Abbott's house?"

Adriel suddenly realized that it was Arielle's voice, but her mouth wasn't moving. He was shocked, but he didn't want to startle her so he responded to her.

Adriel said with a raspy voice, "Yes, mother wants us to get everyone on this end of the road and head back. Their house is the last stop."

It was the first time he spoke that morning since he had gotten up. Arielle didn't react to him responding to her using her telepathy. She figured he knew what she was doing by now because he had written the letter for him and he responded without reacting to her.

Arielle grabbed Adriel's hand tighter as they reached the front gate. Adriel wondered if she knew that he could hear her thoughts, without her using sign language, but she seemed to be ok with it. He didn't want to make a scene, but they were approaching Mr. Abbott's house.

Mr. Abbott wasn't a friendly man. Charles had told Adriel many stories about how he yelled at his stepmother. They approached Mr. Abbott while he was working on his truck in the garage.

Adriel said, "Good morning Mr. Abbott."

Mr. Abbott turned around and picked up his red rag and wiped his hands off.

Arielle slowed down and got behind Adriel as Mr. Abbott approached out from the garage.

Mr. Abbott spoke with a deep groan, "Yeah, what about it."

"Our kitten Dexter got out a few days ago, and we're going door to door to see if anyone has seen him. We're also asking if you can put up our flyers on a fence or mailbox to help with our search until he comes home."

Adriel lifted the flyer to show Mr. Abbott, but he turned his head up to the sun.

Mr. Abbott said, "Well, I don't care much about no feline, but you can put it on the outer fence over there," with a snarl. He pointed at the far end of the property where the road meets the fork by the stop sign.

Adriel looked at the intersection and back at Mr. Abbott and said, "Ok, thanks bunches," with a smile.

As Mr. Abbott walked away, Adriel asked, "Do you think?"

"No!" Mr. Abbott snapped at Adriel before he could ask if Charles could come over. Mr. Abbott didn't like Adriel for some reason, but he knew it was wrong to say nasty words to a child.

Mr. Abbott continued, "Charles is on punishment for going in my things. I caught him using my slingshot in the backyard shooting cans the other day. He can come by sometime next week. Now when you hang that up, use that there stapler you have. That tape will peel my paint right on-off. Ya hear?"

"Yes Sir," Adriel said and they walked.

Adriel couldn't believe what he heard when Mr. Abbott had said about the slingshot. Why would Charles lie to him? They are best friends. As Adriel walked down the road, he looked up at Charles' window. He saw him standing in the window, but he also saw Mr. Abbott watching him and Arielle walking away. Charles waved at him and Adriel smiled but didn't wave back. He knew if he did, he would somehow get Charles into trouble.

As they reached their house there was a car they hadn't seen before. Their parents were already in the house. Adriel opened the front door and a tall slender woman was sitting in the recliner with her legs crossed. Adriel was thinking to himself, my parents were laughing and talking with this woman as if they were friends. I've never seen this woman before. She had dirty blonde hair and she wore glasses. She had a light blue pants suit on in the summertime, which was pretty strange because it was too hot for a suit. As soon as Adriel heard her accent, he realized who she was.

Arielle clinched tight to his hand and hid behind him just like she did at the Abbott's residence.

He held his other hand out to shake hers and said, "Hello, I'm Adriel and this little one behind me is Arielle. She is the shy one in the family."

Adriel moved out of the way to try to have Arielle step out.

She kept moving behind him when Dr. Pavlovsky stooped down to meet her.

Dr. Pavlovskly said, "Don't worry Arielle, we will become good friends," and smiled at her.

Arielle didn't move from behind Adriel.

Dr. Pavlovsky asked when Adeena would be arriving and started to explain the way she liked to set the meeting for that day. She stated she would like to have thirty minutes with the entire family first, to get a feel of how everyone was together and thirty minutes with the parents together. After she assesses the parents, she will take them separately to make sure she was fairly assessing their children without the parents. Both Daniela and Marcus will have to sign a document stating that her sessions were approved by them.

Immediately as she finished discussing that, Adeena walked in the door yelling, "Whose flashy car is that in our driveway?"

Dr. Pavlovsky stood up, introduced herself to Adeena, and told her why she was there. She informed her to have a seat and she explained the details again.

Adeena interrupted her. She stood in the middle of the floor in shock and then belted out, "How is this any of my fault? She is the crazy one, not me," as she pointed to Arielle.

Daniela apologized to the doctor and Marcus grabbed Adeena, took her into the kitchen to talk to her.

Dr. Pavlovsky informed Daniela that this happens all the time. She asked if Daniela could explain why Adeena is blaming the young one.

As Daniela starts explaining, Adriel noticed that the doctor was placing out coloring books and crayons on the coffee table. They were all different types. Arielle picked up the unicorn book and starts coloring.

Adriel started to pay it no mind at first. He turned back to listen to what the doctor was saying until the doctor looked over at him and asked, "Can you check on your father and sister for me please and have them meet back with us in five minutes?"

Adriel then realized she was causing a distraction.

Arielle ran to Adriel as he entered the room to show him what she colored.

"It's beautiful," he said.

Arielle ripped the picture out of the book and handed it to him.

Dr. Pavlovsky looked at him and said, "You two have quite some bound there I see."

Adriel didn't respond. He was starting to understand she was looking into this family and not just Adeena. He also noticed that she wrote in her notepad every time someone did or didn't do something when she spoke to them.

At this time Adeena and their father came back into the room and she was much calmer.

Dr. Pavlovsky went over the plan again and told them that she will go over her assessment. She will get back to the parents the following week if she feels that she will proceed with taking them on for therapy.

The session started and Adriel noticed that the doctor pulled a strange object out of her bag. It was black and shaped like a triangle with lines in the middle of it. It had a metal stick in the center. She did something on the side of it and the metal stick started moving and it had a swooshing sound, like a heartbeat. Adriel was curious what it was, but he had a feeling it wasn't a good thing for him to pay attention to it.

Both Arielle and Adeena became silent. He knew something was wrong when Adeena's face was not angry anymore and Arielle stopped coloring. His mother and father were engaged in the conversation with Dr. Pavlovsky during the whole thirty minutes. Adriel was watching Arielle and Adeena making sure they were okay.

Once the thirty minutes were up, he realized that the doctor didn't ask any of them any questions.

Adriel said, "I thought this was supposed to be a family interaction where you ask us questions together?"

The doctor looked at him, smiled, and said, "I thought I did ask you something, my child, but you never answered me so I kept talking to your parents."

Her smile went away. She was trying to figure out why he wasn't affected. She turned off the metronome.

Slowly Adriel noticed his sisters sat back up from a slouched position moving their bodies away from its direction. Arielle went back to coloring and Adeena looked confused.

The doctor talked to the parents alone, which to Adriel didn't make any sense being he knew that she had already done that. No one else seemed to be paying attention to it. She finished with the parents and called Adriel in.

He told her what she wanted to hear, but she didn't use the metronome this time, which he thought was weird. She didn't ask him any questions about Adeena. She only wanted to know about Arielle and what happened with the cats. None of it made any sense to Adriel. When she asked about Arielle's imaginary friend, he didn't tell her. He knew it would make things worse for Arielle.

When he was done, he went over to Arielle and told her to not tell the weird lady anything about Sunshine. No matter what she says or does, to keep that to herself. Arielle promised him. They pinky swore, played tag with Peppa until Adeena was done and it was Arielle's turn.

It was Arielle's turn. Arielle sat down on the floor and there were no coloring books or crayons on the coffee table this time. Arielle got up from the floor and went to the far end of the couch and sat down.

The doctor tilted her head and said, "Are you afraid of me Arielle?"

Arielle didn't answer her. She just looked at her and clenched her hands tightly.

Dr. Pavlovsky got up from the chair and sat in another chair directly across from Arielle.

She said, "You know I am here because your mother and father think that I can help. They think there are some bad things happening in the house. Do you think there are some bad things happening?"

Arielle looked down at the floor. She was remembering Miles dying and Dexter had gone missing, but was that bad?

The doctor said to her, "Arielle, I think you know something and you would like to tell me but, you are scared to say. Hopefully, we can become friends soon. I am not a bad person. I am a good person, and I can help you."

Suddenly, the shadow with the blue eyes showed up behind the doctor. Arielle looked up and she opened her mouth to speak. As soon as she was going to say something, Peppa started barking outside.

Dr. Pavlovsky said, "Wow that dog is rambunctious, how can you deal with that?"

Arielle closed her mouth and looked outside. Her brother was standing there with Peppa. He looked at her and she looked back. She smiled and the doctor closed the door and the shadow was gone.

As the session went on the doctor couldn't get Arielle to open up. The doctor had the family come back in and told them thank you for having her over and she would contact them early next week to let them know what she came up with.

Adriel looked over at Arielle and she winked at him. He smiled and looked back at the doctor.

The doctor looked at him and said, "Stay safe and have a wonderful summer all of you." The parents walked her to the car.

Adriel went to Arielle and asked her, "What did you say to her?" Arielle used her telepathy, "I didn't say anything. When Peppa barked I saw you and remembered to stay quiet. She told me that I know that something bad is happening here, but I didn't."

Adriel started to think to himself, "I'm the only one that knows what's going on, not Arielle. Why would the doctor think that she does, unless Adeena was talking about Sunshine? Something doesn't add up." He looked at Arielle and gave her a high five and said, "Good job."

Chapter 4
Transformation

Summer rain smells funny, Arielle was thinking as she sat on her bed playing with her dolls. She wished she could be outside by her favorite tree instead, but they have to stay in today. Peppa got up off the floor by the window where she was taking in the air and went to lick Arielle's nose. Arielle wondered why dogs did the weirdest things. She then thought about the dream she have every night and why again she woke up with the pain in her wrist. In the dream, an evil monster was pulling her by her wrist to this dark place. She was kicking and screaming to get away from him. She would look back and see this luminescent light. It felt like she was drawn to it, but she could never get to there. Eventually, the monster would let go and she would wake up in pain.

Every night she kept waking up with the same problem. Peppa was growling at the door, but she never saw anything. The only difference was this time, there was a slight red mark on the side of her wrist, like a burn. It was still hurting a bit. She wore a long-sleeve t-shirt so no one could see it this time.

Later that day, Adeena asked her mother if she could go to Sasha's to hang out for a while?

Daniela looked outside then looked back at her and smiled at her.

She said, "I don't think the weatherman said the rain was letting up today," and then laughed.

Adeena turned and walked away without saying anything to her mother. She went into the living room to sit on the couch and watch TV with her brother. Within ten minutes, an outburst came from the living room,

"Ouch! Get off of me you psycho," Adriel yelled.

Daniela ran into the living room finding Adeena on top of Adriel attacking him. Daniela went over and pulled her off of him.

Daniela yells, "Adeena get a hold of yourself," while she struggled to get Adeena to calm down.

Adeena was growling at Adriel.

Adriel said to his mother, "She was on the couch over there looking outside and I changed the channel. A car drove by with a horn blasting and all of sudden she came over attacking me, hitting me on my head."

Adeena finally calmed down and their mother let her go. Adeena walked over to sit down with a blank look on her face.

Her mother said to her, "What is going on with you child?"

Adeena replied, "Nothing. I was watching that." She leaned back in the chair; crossed her legs as if nothing ever happened.

Adriel left and went upstairs to his room and slammed the door.

Daniela scolded her, "Attacking your brother is not how you get your voice heard in this house. You will not be putting your hands on anyone else. Understand me? You will not be going outside for a week. Go to your room!"

Adeena casually walked upstairs and went to her room.

Daniela called Marcus to tell him what happened. She couldn't believe that Adeena was so calm afterward. Marcus told her he would try to get more out of her when he got home. Daniela wanted to wait until they talked to the doctor, and he agreed.

The next morning Peppa was asleep on the foot of Arielle's bed and suddenly Peppa awakens to see a shadow approaching in the corner of her room. Arielle was having another bad dream. This time she was sweating and fighting. The sheets were halfway kicked off of her. Peppa started to growl as the figure approached Arielle's bed. Peppa leaped off the bed towards the figure and it backed away. Arielle squealed which made Peppa whimper and Peppa backed up towards the window.

Suddenly, Arielle gripped her chest and she couldn't move. Peppa starts growling again and Arielle awakens. Peppa comes back to the bed and starts to lick Arielle's face to make her feel better. Arielle grabs her wrist as it was hurting much worse this time. Peppa whimpered and put her head on Arielle's lap. Arielle was becoming scared. She realizes now that her nightmares are getting worse. She knows she can't keep the markings on her wrist a secret much longer. She gets up to get ready for the day.

Downstairs, Adeena was already up bright and early that Saturday morning and had fixed breakfast for everyone. There was French toast, sausage, eggs, and grits. She made coffee for mother and father and had orange juice ready for Arielle and Adriel.

When her mother walked into the kitchen, she was smiling from ear to ear.

Daniela walked over and kissed her on her forehead and said, "Thank you, sweetheart. What is this lovely occasion for?"

Adeena said, "Oh nothing, I just felt like cooking this morning. So, eat up."

Adeena sat down and started eating before her mother could say anything else.

About ten minutes later, Arielle came down and saw the food. Her mother told her that Adeena made it.

Arielle was ecstatic and signed, "Wow, thanks!"

Adeena didn't respond. She got up from the table and dumped her plate, which wasn't finished. She had a very disgusted look on her face and walked off. Their mother noticed and watched Adeena as she walked off. When she got to the stairs, Adriel was coming down.

She said, "Hey I fixed breakfast for you twin. Hope you enjoy it."

He looked at her oddly as she walked pass and went into her room. He got a bowl of cereal instead.

Daniela whispered to him, "You shouldn't have done that. She worked hard on this."

Adriel didn't respond. He looked over at Arielle and noticed that she had his old sweatband on her wrist that he had made for her.

He laughed and said, "Wow I see you are wearing my old sweatband. It finally fits your tiny little wrist."

She slowly moved her arm off the table and kept eating her food.

Adriel started to wonder why she didn't respond.

Later that morning, they piled in the vehicle to go see Grandma Pearl. Daniela asked Adeena what she wanted to listen to on the radio.

Adeena replied, "Whatever you want mother, it doesn't bother me one bit."

Her mother looked over at Marcus and back at the rest of the kids and said, "Well okay then."

She started the vehicle and turned it to a station that played the current music to please everyone in the car. She felt like Adeena was making progress for the day and deserved to hear what she thought she liked.

When they reached the retirement home, Adeena seemed to get a little agitated and Adriel could see it. He knew if he told his parents they would blow it off because he saw how the morning went with breakfast.

They got out of the vehicle and for some reason, Adeena stood right beside him. She hadn't done that since they were in school. He felt very uneasy. He moved away from her and as soon as he did that she growled. He walked over to Arielle and took her hand. When they got to Grandma Pearl's room, Arielle and Adriel ran up to Grandma Pearl and left Adeena to come in on her own. Adeena stood outside her door alone.

Grandma Pearl realized she hadn't come in and said, "My dear, why are you lurking in the shadows like a monster, get in here and hug your grandma."

Adeena looked like a big dark shadow had covered her up out in the hallway. Arielle had crouched behind Adriel.

As soon as she came into the room, her face changed into a smile. Adeena's eyes were on Adriel and Arielle as she walked over to Grandma Pearl.

She said, "Hola Abuela, how are you feeling?" She never hugged her. She stood in front of her talking. Everyone noticed that something was off, but they tried to not bring attention to it for Grandma Pearl's sake.

Adeena was Grandma Pearl's favorite and for her to not show any affection was very suspicious. Grandma Pearl started to notice.

Daniela pulled Grandma Pearl over to the side and said, "Madre let me get you over to the chair. Would you like to sit in your chair?"

"Yes dear," Grandma Pearl looked back at Adeena confused.

Marcus pulled Adeena aside and asked her, "Are you okay, this is unusual behavior for you."

Adeena smiled and said, "Whatever do you mean," and then she walked over to the kitchen table to sit down.

Marcus looked at Adriel and shook his head. They all went into the living room and talked to Grandma Pearl.

While the rest of the family was laughing and spending time with Grandma Pearl, Adeena was steadily staring at Adriel and Arielle with a smile on her face. As she watched Adriel, Adeena was steaming on the inside with fury about Arielle being attached to his side.

Grandma Pearl turned to Adeena at the end of the visit and said, "Princesa, can you come and give me a hug before you leave?"

Adeena got up and said, "Love you too Abuela," and she opened the door and walked out.

Daniela gasped and covered her mouth in shock.

Marcus apologized and ran after her.

Adriel and Arielle gave Grandma Pearl their hugs and kisses. Grandma Pearl started to tear up. Daniela kept her company a few minutes more to get her calm.

As they were coming out of the building, Adriel saw their father scolding Adeena in the parking lot.

He thought, "She didn't care, it's useless."

He leaned down and motioned for Arielle to put her headphones in.

Adeena saw Adriel and Arielle and she tried to walk away from her father, but he pulled her back and she pushed him. Marcus grabbed her arm and told her to never do that again. She smacked him and started screaming. Adriel ran to aid his father and Arielle followed behind.

As Arielle approached, she saw the shadow again at the end of the parking that made her stop in her tracks. Fear overwhelmed her as she watched it come closer to her. It reached out to grab her, but once it touched her, she was scooped up. Her headphones dropped out of her ears as she spun around. Arielle had no idea what had just happened. She thought the shadow had taken her.

When she opened her eyes, she saw that she was lying on the ground with her mother. Daniela had her in her arms lying on the ground. Arielle noticed a car was at least a foot from them. There were people all around hovering over them, talking and yelling. Arielle looked over her shoulder and she saw her mother close her eyes as she started to let her go. Marcus ran over to pick her up.

Later at the hospital, Daniela slowly opened her eyes, but all she saw were bright lights. She tried to reach her face with her right hand and noticed that she couldn't move it. She realized she had a cast on her arm. So, she looked over to her left and saw her son was asleep in a chair with Arielle on his lap.

Arielle hopped off his lap and skipped out of the room. Adriel woke up and saw his mother was awake. He came to her side and hugged her. He apologized to her for leaving Arielle behind and causing the accident.

She consoled him and told him, it was not his fault and it was okay.

Marcus came in and he laid his hand on Adriel's shoulder and said with a stern voice, "Son, none of this is your fault."

Adriel looked up at him and he started to apologize to him as well.

His father stopped him and said, "Look, you can't save everyone. If Adeena wasn't trying to make everyone miserable, you wouldn't have to feel like you needed to split yourself in half. She feels terrible right now. I think you should talk to her."

At that moment Adriel became infuriated. He turned and punched the wall.

His parents both yelled, "Adriel!"

Adriel was angry and said, "If she hadn't snapped at dad and hit him, I wouldn't have tried to come across the parking lot. Mom wouldn't have had to save Arielle and she wouldn't be in this bed. How could this not be her fault? Every day she keeps trying to start things in the house and you want me to go talk to her. No! No, I will not!"

He waved his hands back and forth and shook his head.

Daniela turned to Marcus as he was about to say something to Adriel and stopped him.

She said, "Let him cool off for the moment. This is fresh."

She looked back at Adriel with concern and told him to sit back down.

Marcus agreed, kissed her on the cheek, and told her that he would be out in the waiting room with the kids while they waited on the doctor.

That night, Adriel woke up to use the bathroom and he heard someone entering his mother's room. He thought it was a doctor or a nurse checking on her. He didn't hear the normal shuffling, but he did hear his mother moan and the heart monitor peeping faster. He washed his hands and came out of the bathroom. He looked around and didn't see anyone. He looked at his mother and she seemed fine. He went to the door and opened it, but there was no one in the hallway. So, he went to sit back in the chair and turned his iPod on, but the battery was low. He didn't have his charger, so he went to the waiting room to get it out of the bag that his father had brought.

Adriel walked back towards his mother's room. He saw the lights were dimmer by his mother's room. He knew something wasn't right because there was nothing wrong when he left the room. He decided to walk faster and as he got closer the lights came back on. He opened the door and his mother's heart monitor was beeping loudly and her face looked like she had seen a ghost. When he got closer to her, the nurses and doctors flew in the get to her.

They pushed him aside and wheeled her out of the room. Adriel ran to wake his father up.

He blurted out, "Something just happened to mother. I don't know what happened. I came down here to get my charger and when I got back her heart monitor was beeping loudly and the doctors took her out."

His father got up and didn't say a word. He went to the nurses' desk to find out what was wrong.

"I don't think I should've left the room when I heard it go off the first time. I should've told the nurses about," Adriel told his father as his father paced back and forth in the waiting room.

Marcus wasn't listening to him at the moment. All he could think about was that she needs to be okay. After an hour had passed, the doctor came to Marcus and pulled him aside. Marcus shook his hand and the doctor placed his hand on his shoulder. He thanked him and walked away.

Marcus came over to the kids and told them that their mother will be fine. They are going to keep her for another day as she had a seizure. They have to make sure that she doesn't have another one.

Adeena folded her arms and turned away.

Arielle came over to Adriel and sat in his lap. He heard what she was thinking as he did before.

So he whispered, "That means mother will come home soon, but she will be sick for a while."

Marcus walked over to Adriel and laid his hand on his shoulder, grabbed him gently then walked away. Adriel didn't know what it meant, but he could tell that his father was in agony.

Chapter 5
Who Are You

As she lay looking out the window holding her wrist, a tear fell from her eye. Peppa was lying on her lap looking up at Arielle. She had another nightmare, but this time when Arielle woke up, she saw something leaving her room. Her door wasn't open and it scared her. She couldn't explain what it was. She saw Peppa was over by the window growling as it was leaving. She had another mark on her wrist. She wondered if she should tell her brother, but she didn't know what to say.

Just then, Sunshine appeared, which made her smile. They talked about her day and she began to tell Sunshine about what she saw.

Sunshine told her to not worry, that it is nothing to be afraid of. Fear was part of growing up and that she shouldn't let it get to her. She was becoming a big girl and she is strong. Sunshine changed the subject and asked her what she was going to do for the day.

Arielle mentioned that she had to help Adriel with taking care of their mother since she was home from the hospital.

Sunshine said, "Today is going to be hard for you, but don't worry, Adriel is a good brother and he will always be there for you."

Arielle got up and put on the sweatband. She went down for breakfast, but no one had fixed anything for her. She saw there was a mess in the sink from someone fixing something. She went back upstairs to go to Adriel's room and he wasn't there. She went to Adeena's room and she was still sleeping. She closed her door and went to her parent's room and saw Adriel feeding their mother her breakfast. She asked Adriel about breakfast.

He said, "Oh sorry kiddo, I totally forgot to make extra. Can you eat some cereal today? I will make sure you have some lunch."

She went back down, climbed on the counter, got the cereal, and then got the milk from the refrigerator. She then realized that the bowl was a little more complicated to get. She looked over at Peppa and grumbled.

Sunshine appeared and pointed to the chairs at the table. She walked over and scooted the chair to the counter. She climbed into the chair. The chair started to wobble a bit as she stood up in it. Peppa whined nervously. When she opened the cabinet door, the shadow appeared in the room at the same time.

When Adeena entered the room, Arielle reached for the bowl and the shadow startled her. Arielle could see the shadow from the corner of her eye and she screamed. Adeena also saw the shadow from where she was standing in the entry of the kitchen and she froze. Arielle fell off the chair and Peppa barked.

This made Adriel run down the stairs to see what happened. When he entered, Adeena was still frozen from seeing the shadow. By this time the shadow had disappeared. He picked Arielle up off the floor. Her sweatband had slipped off her wrist and Peppa brought it to her. Adriel saw it and noticed what was on her wrist.

He asked her, "What happened?"

She wouldn't answer him. She grabbed her wrist and turned from him.

Adeena said, "Did you see it, please tell me you saw it this time?"

He looked at her confused and shook his head.

Adeena ran off to her room while he sat there on the floor holding Arielle.

Adriel took Arielle to their mother's room to let her eat her cereal.

He said, "I figured if I have my eyes on both of you, I don't think anything will happen to you while I am here."

Arielle smiled and looked at her mother. Even though she could see her mother still looked the same, she knew she wasn't.

Daniela looked at Adriel in shame while he fed her breakfast.

Adriel said, "What's wrong mother?"

She replied, "I never thought I would have my child doing this for me."

Adriel replied, "Don't worry; you will be back on your feet in no time. The doctor said this is only temporary. Your seizures will calm down and you will get your hands back."

Arielle felt bad that she was part of her mother's problem, but their father told them it wasn't their fault. She knew if the shadow would stop coming around, maybe her mother would be fine. She felt if her brother could just see it, maybe he could help her get rid of it somehow.

"Arielle darling," Daniela said, "Why are you looking so confused?"

Arielle was surprised by her mother's question.

Adriel tries not to think about anything while Arielle signs, "Nothing mother."

Adriel interrupts, "I told her to come and help with my daily duties and be my little helper, but I haven't given her any chores yet," with a goofy smile.

Their mother looked back at Arielle and said, "Well that sounds great. I hope you don't make her do too much, she is young and it is summertime. Neither one of you should be doing all of this alone. I did tell your father a nurse is better. This isn't fair to any of you."

He covered up Arielle's wrist on the way out of the room and went to the bathroom to talk about her wrist.

Adriel closed the door and she sat on the toilet.

He said, "Arielle, I love you, but you need to tell me what's going on."

She used her telepathy, "I don't know what it is. I have nightmares and it hurts me."

Adriel was perplexed, "Who hurts you?"

She thought, "It hurts me, the shadow. It comes in my nightmares, I think. I think it hurts our mother too."

Adriel fell back on the wall and dropped to the floor with his hands on his face. "What are you saying, Arielle?"

She shrugged her shoulders and looked at the floor.

"Are you saying that this wasn't a person that drove that car into our mother," Adriel asked.

She thought about it before she answered, "No. I saw it when you ran to father. It came to me. I didn't see a car. Every time I see it, bad things happen. I saw it today when I fell out of the chair. I saw it when Adeena fell off the lawnmower. I saw it the day she hit you. I saw it the day Miles died and when I picked out Dexter."

"What," whispered Adriel?

He continues, "So, is it your imaginary friend Sunshine?"

She started crying. She knew that Sunshine was still there, but something happened after he left. She got up, turned around with her arms folded, and thought, "Sunshine is still around."

Adriel tried to figure out how either of them have anything to do with the accidents or deaths. It didn't make sense to him. He knew something was off and he knew that someone was doing something to his little sister. He had to figure out why she was talking about a shadow. Then he remembered something. Adeena did say she saw something when they were in the kitchen. He took Arielle back to his mother's room.

He said, "Hey mother, what do you want to watch on TV this morning? Arielle, sit here and watch over our mother. I will be right back."

He turns the TV on and heads down the hallway to Adeena's room.

Adeena was in her closet looking for something when Adriel entered the room.

He closed the door and said, "Adeena, what were you talking about in the kitchen?"

Adeena popped out of the closet with a smile on her face and said, "You saw it didn't you?"

Adriel shook his head and said, "Adeena please I need you to be serious right now. What were you talking about? There is something I am trying to figure out and I need your input on it. So, what were you talking about?"

Adeena was puzzled by this, but replied, "Wait, why, what's going on? What are you looking into?"

She realizes he wasn't in her room about her; he came for someone else's interest.

He says, "Something is going on in this house and you said you saw something. I need to know what you saw."

Adriel knew that he had to be vague because she was very suspicious and to get his answers, he couldn't have her playing games.

Adeena was very pleased to see he cared. She told him that she believed the shadowy figure was Sunshine. She remembered him to be known under a different name. She was looking in her closet for something she had when she was younger. She used to have an imaginary friend, but she never told him about it.

Adriel was shocked to hear about it because they shared everything. He asked her if she believed it to be Sunshine, why didn't she tell him before now.

Adeena said, "Well first, I needed to make sure I was correct. I didn't know you couldn't see it and being that I and Arielle could I wasn't sure it was the same thing."

Adriel sat down on her bed in disbelief. He couldn't believe that Arielle was telling the truth.

He asked her, "Why did you attack me the other day?"

She looked at him in shame and said, "I honestly don't know. Something came over me. I felt like something was controlling me and I could see myself doing it, but I couldn't stop."

He didn't know what to say to her, because he thought about what Arielle had told him. He also didn't want to take the chance that Adeena was lying.

Adriel said, "Keep looking for the name of your imaginary friend and let's figure out how to fix this."

Adeena agreed and he left to go back to their mother's room.

Later that day, the phone rang as Marcus entered from work. He answers, "Hello. This is her husband. I'm sorry, she can't come to the phone, Mrs. Pavlovsky. She had an accident. Yes, she is okay for now, but unfortunately, she is healing and I will be tending to all the business with the children. How can I help you?"

As Mrs. Pavlovsky informs him of the outcome of the visit, Adriel ran downstairs to see who his father was on the phone with. He saw his father's expression and it wasn't pleasant.

Marcus looked up and saw Adriel standing there and he turned to avoid eye contact with Adriel.

He responded to Mrs. Pavlovsky, "Well I don't approve of that and we only are looking for Adeena for counseling at this time. Unfortunately, if you are looking for more than that we will have to decline at this time."

Adriel was very curious. Why would she want another person and who else?

Marcus responds again, "Well Mrs. Pavlovsky, or Doctor, whatever. If you aren't satisfied with that, then I'm sorry. Adeena only and that is final. Have a good day." Then he hung up.

Marcus turned around and grabbed his beard.

Adriel leaned on the wall and was shocked about the call.

"Adriel," his father called. He knew Adriel was still there.

Adriel slowly came into the living room, "Yes sir," Adriel replied.

"You speak nothing of what you heard, understand me," his father said.

"Yes sir," Adriel replied with confidence.

His father asked him what happened with his mother and his siblings. He only told him about the chores and attending to his mother. He didn't tell him what he found out. He knew now that with Dr. Pavlovsky wanting another person, this was more than he would have to investigate. Adriel informed his father what he had sat out to cook for dinner. He told him the laundry was in the dryer and Adeena did the other half already. His father thanked him and told him to get Adeena to come and help him with dinner.

Adeena was already on her way down the stairs before Adriel could go and get her.

She said, "I heard him yelling so don't worry."

He went to their mother, she asked, "Is everything okay?"

He came in and he glanced over at his mother.

He waved his hand and said, "Everything is okay," Adriel lowered his head so he wouldn't have to look at his mother

He continued, "It was just one of those phone calls that irritate father."

She didn't believe him.

She said "I heard him say Dr. Pavlovksy's name. Don't lie to me, Adriel Gibson."

Daniela knew her son was lying to her because he couldn't look at her and she heard her husband. She repeated herself with a stern voice, "Adriel, is everything okay?"

Adriel looked up at her and said, "I promised father I wouldn't say anything."

She nodded her head and told him okay. Daniela knew that she would have to go to the source for answers because her son was honorable.

That evening after everyone was settled and had gone to bed, Daniela looked over to her husband and she said, "Adriel is a good kid. He did a great job with his siblings today. He fixed me breakfast and helped Arielle. She fell when she tried to get herself breakfast, but he helped her get right back up again. Then, later he taught her how to help him do everything for me. Now, he and Adeena are talking again. What I don't get is how my husband would use his loyalty against him to keep things from his mother."

Marcus let out a big sigh, turned to her, and said, "He told you, didn't he?"

She said angrily, "No. Our loyal son didn't break his word with you, but what I don't get is why you made him do it? How could you? I am your wife Marcus. What was the phone call about with Dr. Pavlovsky? I could hear you up here yelling at her."

Marcus shook his head and said, "Honey I am so sorry. I didn't want you getting as upset as I did and having another seizure. Promise me if I tell you that you won't get upset?"

She took a deep breath and said, "I will not get upset."

Marcus sat down on the bed and said, "She wants to counsel Arielle and Adeena. She said that both of them have problems and they both need counseling. Arielle is seeing imaginary friends and that she needs to project her feelings onto realistic things. Adeena, however, is blaming Arielle's imaginary friend for her problems. I told her that she needs to only see Adeena as Arielle isn't the problem."

Daniela looked up at the ceiling, took another deep breath, and blew it out.

She calmly said, "Thank you, thank you very much, sweetheart."

Daniela lay her head back on the pillow for a brief moment to think about what he said. A minute goes by and she turns back to him and says, "Why would she want Arielle when she knows that Arielle has Down Syndrome and it is hard for her to make friends. That doesn't make sense to me."

Marcus leaned over to her and said in a whisper, "She stated that Adriel and Arielle need to separate their relationship. She is dependent on her brother too much. She will never release her imaginary friend if he is around."

"What! Okay, that woman has issues. I don't know if I even want Adeena to see her," Daniela said angrily.

Marcus hugged and patted her back.

He said, "Honey, calm down. Take a breath. You have to stay calm. Remember?"

He had to keep her calm before they went to bed. They stayed up watching TV for a few hours and then went to sleep.

During the night, Adriel had another dream where he saw Adeena with blood on her face and screaming, "No Charles, Stop," but he saw it as if he was Charles this time. He woke up in a sweat. He couldn't figure it out. He got up and went to use the bathroom. As he came out, he heard a big crash coming from Arielle's room. He ran to her room and he opened the door. He looked over and he saw Peppa whimpering. The window had broken with glass all around her. She had a big piece of glass stuck on the side of her and she was bleeding. He looked over to see if he saw

Arielle, but she was still asleep so he went to aid Peppa. When he bent over to pick her up, she growled. He thought she was growling at him. He turned around and didn't see anything.

Arielle began crying and fighting in her sleep. Adriel ran to her bedside, but he got knocked to the floor by something blocking his way. He got back up and tried to go to her again. Peppa started barking heavily. Adriel turned back around and grabs Arielle.

He says, "Wake up Arielle."

While Adriel is waking her up, Peppa gets herself to her feet and limps to the door. The door slams close before she can get out. Adriel looks at the door then Peppa starts to bark again at the door. Their father comes to the door to try to open it, but he can't.

Adriel is holding Arielle tightly in his arms. He knows now that something was in the room, but he couldn't see it.

He yells, "Sunshine, if you can hear me, I am getting Arielle out of here and I need you to let us go."

Their father was still trying to open the door. He couldn't hear what was going on in the room. He only knew that the door was locked when it slammed closed and he couldn't open it. He banged on the door with his fist.

He yells, "Adriel are you in there? Open the door son."

Adriel walked over with Arielle in his arms and tried to open the door.

He yelled again, "Sunshine, I know you hear me and I know you are hurting my sister, but if you love her, please let her go so that she can be safe. She is your friend. Please let us leave now."

Suddenly, the door opened and their father saw Adriel holding Arielle in his arms in the middle of her bedroom floor. Arielle woke up and there was another mark on her wrist, but this time her wrist was broken. Peppa lay by the door bleeding. Their father saw Adriel holding Ariel and she was holding her wrist crying. He then looked down at Peppa and she was bleeding. He was confused. Their father picked Peppa up.

Marcus looked at Adriel and asked him, "What happened?"

Adriel said, "I will explain it to you on the way to the hospital. Let's take care of them first."

They took Peppa to the vet and Arielle to the hospital. Adriel explained to their father the best way he could what he knew about what was going on.

Chapter 6
My Name

Adeena was to stay with their mother and take care of her while their father and Adriel were tending to Arielle at the hospital that night. Adeena couldn't sleep because she was trying to figure out what her imaginary friend's name was. She was pacing in her room the whole night. By morning, she reached back into her memory when she first encountered the shadowy figure and remembered having conversations with it. She first remembered talking to something that was much more pleasant than the shadow. As her mind drifted back to that moment, she sat on the floor a vision formed in her mind from when she was a child.

Adeena saw this bright image in front of her with a smile on its face. It told her that it has a friend that would come to see her in a few moments. It had been trying to be friends with her for a while now and she was resisting too much, but she was a strong soldier. All she had to do was take its hand and say, "I am yours and you are mine. Now and forevermore." A second later the shadowy image came to her and she became frightened. She looked for the other being, but it was gone. The shadow reached out with its hand and Adeena didn't move. It leaned down to take her hand and Adeena ran away.

Right at that moment in Adeena's memory, she snapped back. She realized that she had met the shadow when she was Arielle's age. She knew she had to tell Adriel. She found some paper and started to write down everything she could remember from her past. When she was done, she went to fix her mother's breakfast and took it to her. When she got to her mother's room, Adeena noticed that she looked like she was still sleeping. Adeena nudged her and asked if she wanted her breakfast. Her mother slowly turned her head and looked at her strangely. Adeena was puzzled. She wasn't sure what to do.

She asked again, "Mother, do you want me to feed you your breakfast?"

Her mother again looked at her strangely and then turned her head back over to the other side of the room.

Adeena looked up and saw what her mother was looking at. The closet door was cracked open. The cloth hangers were moving, but there was no wind blowing. Adeena moved the tray out of the way and walked over to the closet and opened the doors wider.

She didn't see anything. So, she closed the doors. She turned to walk back to her mother and then heard the hangers moving again. She stopped and turned around slowly. The closet door opened abruptly. Adeena took a step back. She looked back at her mother.

Daniela had a concerned look on her face.

She said, "Something is in there isn't it, but I can't see what it is."

Adeena immediately realized what it was.

As soon as she thought about it, she saw those glassy blue eyes appear from the dark as the hangers started to spread open. Adeena fell over onto the floor.

Daniela asked, "What is happening? I can't see anything. Adeena get up!"

Adeena crawled across the floor to her mother's bed then she got up onto the bed. She hovered over top of her mother to protect her, but the shadow hovered over top of Adeena. It grabbed her mother's head and squeezed it tightly. Her mother's eyes rolled back and her face shook profusely. Adeena screamed and cried. She pleaded for the shadow to stop.

The shadow looked at Adeena and it held out one hand to her.

She yelled, "No."

Adeena looked up at the shadow with tears in her eyes. Her voice trembling, she asked, "What is your name?"

It responded to her, "You know my name. You have said it many times. You called and cried for me in your nightmares, but you will not come with me. Why?"

Adeena turned back around grabbed her mother, held her tightly, and cried as the shadow finally let go of her mother. It drifted off into the closet then disappeared. Daniela stopped convulsing and her eyes closed. She fell into a deep sleep and Adeena called her father on the phone and told them what happened.

When Marcus and Adriel returned, Adriel went to get Adeena. Adeena asked him if their father believed him about the shadow.

Adriel said, "Father thinks that we are making this up and that we need to grow up. He thinks that our mother is having seizures and that we are traumatized by this whole thing. He believes that I'm too close to Arielle. That I broke the window to make it look like something happened to Peppa and that I hurt Arielle. So, don't try and convince him about the shadow anymore because he has heard enough of it. He also thinks we need to own up to our responsibilities. He told me that they have too much on their plate and there is way too much horse playing going on in the house."

Adeena got so infuriated about what Adriel told her. She got up and kicked the wall.

She said, "That's not fair. I know what I saw. You believe me, right?"

Adriel sighed and said, "Look I didn't see anything, but I know something is hurting our mother and Arielle. Something definitely hurt Peppa. What happened earlier, because he wouldn't tell me anything?"

Adeena told him what she saw and then she pulled out her notebook to read it to him. The one thing she couldn't remember was the shadow's name.

Adriel was shocked.

He leaned back on her bed and said, "Woo, how are you seeing the same things that Arielle is seeing. Is this thing going after both of you?"

He paused and then he continued, "Give me a second. I will be right back."

Adriel ran off to his parent's room. He knocked on the door and his father told him to come in. His mother was propped up facing the TV watching her favorite soap opera and she seemed to be okay.

Marcus was brushing her hair and he looked up at Adriel and said, "Yes," in an annoyed voice.

His mother turned around and said, "Hey sweetie with a smile on her face.

Adriel said, "Hey I was coming in to check on you. I heard you had another seizure. You okay?"

She smiled, "Yes, I'm doing okay. I hate those things, hopefully, I don't get anymore. Your sister did a great job. She was terrified though. I guess I have hallucinations with them as well, but I will be okay. How is Arielle, is she resting?"

"She is fine; she is taking a nap right now. The doctor put her on something to help her sleep better," he said with a frown while kicking his foot.

Adriel looked over at his father in a snide way, "Just curious, when you talked to Dr. Pavlovsky, did she ever ask you about Arielle's imaginary friend Sunshine?"

His father stopped brushing her hair and sat up. The hairs on his back were prickled.

His mother said, "Yes. She asked about Sunshine because Adeena told her about it, but I thought it was curious myself being that we were all talking to her first before she had a chance to talk to Adeena. Honey, don't you think that is very strange? I meant to bring that up to you. I can't remember why I forgot about that?"

Marcus was still sitting there stunned and hadn't moved. Adriel was watching him and wanted to ask him about the phone call badly.

Then Adriel said, "So if she already knew about Sunshine, do you think that it is strange that Adeena started attacking us right after she arrived? Then everyone gets hurt and we can't explain anything?"

Daniela laughed. "Adriel, you want to blame all of this on a woman we just met? Come on."

She looked over at her husband who hadn't said a word or moved.

She said, "Honey?"

She was concerned because he was just sitting there.

Adriel walked over to his father and stood in front of him.

Marcus said, "Adriel may be right. When I spoke with her, she told me that Adriel knows too much and he spends too much time with Arielle. When Adeena told me the same thing Adriel did, I knew there couldn't be a chance that they were lying. Then he comes in here telling us about something that he couldn't have known."

His mother looked at Adriel and then back at Marcus. She was still in doubt, shaking her head.

She said, "You are thinking too far into it."

Marcus said, "You didn't hallucinate, you just couldn't see it just like Adriel couldn't when he was in the room with Arielle helping her."

"What," Daniela exclaimed. She continued, "What are the two of you talking about?"

Adriel explains to her what happened to Arielle and then what happened with Adeena when she was Arielle's age. They couldn't figure out what was going on, but they were trying to put the pieces together. They didn't know if it was a ghost, or if it was connected to Sunshine. However, they do know that it was causing pain to them and only Adeena and Arielle can see it.

Daniela wasn't fully convinced that it was some supernatural being, but she knew something was happening to her family and the doctor knew about it.

Daniela said, "Well we need to find out if Dr. Pavlovsky knows about it because her interest in Adeena and Arielle isn't a coincidence."

Adriel was pleased. He had gotten the answer he was looking for.

He said, "Mom you need to relax and, please don't overstress it. I will get with Charles and ride to town tomorrow since he has to go and do errands for his stepmother. Adeena can stay here and help out. I already prepped breakfast and there aren't any house chores to do. Arielle should be okay. I should be back by mid-afternoon to get dinner ready. Father, I will have some information for you by the time you get home."

Adriel headed back to Adeena's room. When he got back, he was so excited to tell her what he knew. He could see she had been pacing again.

She was agitated and said, "Well, tell me."

He shook his head. "Ok, so remember when Dr. Pavlovsky came and we had to do separate sessions with her?"

Adeena asked, "Who?"

Adriel chuckled and said, "The psychiatrist, the one that has the German accent that came to analyze the family for you."

Adeena was confused. She told him that he was crazy and that it never happened.

He realized the metronome that was used must have done something to her. How Adeena and Arielle were out of it when their mother and father were talking to Dr. Pavlovsky. So, he explained everything to her.

Adeena said, "If we go to the library and look it up, can you show me what it looks like?"

Adriel replied, "I will print off a picture of it when I go tomorrow with Charles and bring it to you."

So, he told her how Dr. Pavlovsky knew about her and Arielle being associated with Sunshine and the shadow. Somehow, she brought it up at the appointment, but the doctor tricked their parents into talking about it. She used the machine to trick Adeena into telling the doctor what she wanted to know about Arielle. For some reason, the doctor wants to get a hold of them. He believed the doctor had something to do with both the shadow and Sunshine. Adeena agreed to his plan and they parted for the evening.

As the night progressed, Arielle felt a cool breeze. She sat up in her bed. Sunshine rarely came during the night, but this was a rare occasion.

Arielle smiled, "Hey Sunshine, why are you here tonight," as she rubs her eyes.

Sunshine looked down at her arm and saw that she was hurting and said, "Oh no Arielle, you're hurting. I'm sorry. Your boo-boo will go away soon. I wanted to come to you because I would like you to meet a friend of mine. My friend's name is Baymore. Baymore is here to protect you at night time. Baymore has been trying to come to tell you that, but you have been very afraid. Now that you are without distractions, Baymore thinks this is a good time to meet and you shouldn't be afraid anymore. All you have to do is reach out your hand and say I am yours; you are mine. Now and forevermore. Baymore just wants to be your friend just like you are mine. Do you think you can do that for me?"

Arielle looked at Sunshine unsure of what Sunshine meant by going with Baymore.

Sunshine knew that but ignored it.

Sunshine stood up and said, "I will let Baymore come in so don't be afraid okay. Remember, reach out your hand and say what I told you." Sunshine disappeared.

Arielle looked around her room and didn't see anything. She leaned back on her pillow and as soon as she thought it was over, the shadow came into her room by the door. When she looked into those crystal blue eyes and fear rushed over her as she screamed.

She used her telepathy and called for Adriel, "Adriel, help, help!"

"I am Baymore. Reach out your hand and say the verse, Arielle."

Arielle closed her eyes and cried.

When Adriel heard Arielle's call for him in his head, it woke him up. He ran to her room. He started banging on her door. Adriel couldn't open the door, so he banged on the door with his body.

He yelled, "Arielle, I can't open the door."

As Adriel tried to break the door down, his father came with an ax and told Adriel to move out the way. He started hacking at the door.

Arielle was terrified. Baymore hoovered over top of Arielle, insisting on her to say the lines. She pulled the covers over her head and kept crying!

As Baymore kept insisting on her to say the verse the room was completely covered in darkness. Baymore yanked the blanket off of her.

Baymore yelled at her, "You are mine and you will give me your hand."

Finally, her father and Adriel broke through. When they got into her room, they were amazed by what they saw. The room was filled with black smoke. They couldn't see anything. Baymore looked back at them and vanished. When Baymore vanished, the smoke cleared the room. Arielle jumped up and ran to Adriel.

Marcus said, "This time I could see that"

Adriel said to his father, "Now do you believe."

Adriel asked Arielle, "Did you say it?"

Arielle shook her head no.

They walked out of the room and Adriel kept her in his room for the rest of the night. Marcus sat in her room with the ax on her bed guarding her room hoping that it would come back, but it didn't.

The next morning, Charles and Adriel rode their bikes to town as planned. Adriel was explaining to Charles what happened. Charles was very excited about it, which made Adriel freaked out. This shouldn't have been strange for Adriel, but it was. Adriel shrugged it off. They planned out their path for the day so they can get to Dr. Pavlovksy's office.

First, they decided to go pay the utilities and cable bill at the market. After that, they headed down to the Pharmacy to get his stepmother's prescriptions. The last stop was two doors down from Dr. Pavlovksy's office, which was the Post Office to pick up the mail. Adriel knew he had to be slick about this because it had to be around lunchtime. He needed to make sure she wasn't in the office at that time. So, they waited on the bench down the street from her office to see when she left.

Charles went in to ask for her and Adriel slid behind the door as Charles was talking to the receptionist. He had the receptionist looking for his name on the waiting list. She told him he wasn't on their waiting list. She also asked if he could come back with his parents. He then asked her to look up his name on the computer, that his parents were down the street and he was trying to make sure he had an appointment today or sometime soon. He just didn't want a mix-up of dates as it had happened before. He dropped her pen holder on the floor so that Adriel could go into Dr. Pavlovksy's office unseen.

While Adriel was in her office, Charles was helping her pick up the pens and apologizing to the receptionist. He distracted her while picking up the pens by asking her a lot of questions about getting internships and going to college. Adriel looked in her file cabinets, suitcase, and then in her closet. He found a brown box that had a picture on the top of it that had faces scratched out. The box had a latch on it, with a keyhole. Adriel looked around for something to open it with. He found a safety pin in her desk drawer. Once he opened it, it had bones, a vile of blood and notes in it. He couldn't read the notes because it was another language. He took pictures so he could figure it out later when he went to the library. He put it back and listened at the door for his queue to leave.

Charles saw Adriel's feet at the door.

He said to the receptionist, "Well you're very nice, but I like Pumpernickel."

The receptionist laughed and said, "What in the world does that mean?"

Charles replied, "I don't know," and knocked over her pens again and yelled out, "Dang-it let me help you."

Charles walked over on the side of the desk to block her view of the office and so that she could turn her back. They bent over with their backs toward the door and picked them up. Adriel eased out of the office and ran down the street to the bench. Charles came out five minutes later and they rode on their bikes to the library.

When they got to the library, they gave each other a high five. They had never felt so excited.

Adriel smiled at him and said, "Now comes the hard part."

He showed Charles the picture of the notes. Charles's face showed how baffled he was and he pushed the phone back over to Adriel.

Adriel sat down at the library's computer. He did a search to find out what language the notes were. He learned that the language was German, which to him was no surprise as the doctor was German. He then went through the process of researching the dialogue. He determined it was some sort of biblical terminology for demonic control.

Charles saw him sit back in the chair and asked him what was wrong. Adriel didn't respond, instead, he turned the computer in Charles' direction.

When Charles read the information, he learned that the demon made the kids choose between good and evil at a very young age. The human, also known as the master, who would take control of the demon had to place a portion of their blood with the bone of the demon's vessel and bury them both in the land where the demon was to do the master's bidding. The other portion was to be kept in a safe place. The demon would take two forms. The first form is pleasure. This is to gain trust of the victim and then pain. This one is to inflict misery on them and the surrounding loved ones. The master can use the demon on whomever they please to manipulate them into believing whatever they want.

Once the demon has them under their control, which starts out with pleasure, it will introduce you to the real demon that tortures you. The demon requires you to say a verse for you to be bonded with it, "I am yours; you are mine. Now and forevermore."

This demon is called Baymore, which was the actual demon. If the person accepts the demon's offer, the human soul will then be added to the demon's list bound to Hell forever. If they do not say the verse, but instead say the verse, "You love the light and the light is your own," without any help from the demon, the demon will remove itself from your life and the person will forget the demon ever existed.

Charles looked over at Adriel and said to him, "Dude this is wicked. Is this really what is happening right now?"

Adriel asked Charles if there was a picture of the demon. He scrolled down on the screen and there it was. Charles jumped out of his seat and said, "No freaking way dude. I've been seeing that thing since I was a little kid. Are you saying that I have been dealing with the same thing in my house all the time? Every time my dad hits my stepmother it shows up."

Adriel shook his head and said, "I'm sorry man, we gotta stop this thing. Let's see if there is a way to stop it."

They read that if they could find where the master buried both sets of bones, they would have to sacrifice and bury everything with the one that they love.

They looked at each other and both of them said it out loud, "Someone you love?"

Charles wondered to himself, who did he have in common that they could sacrifice to get rid of this demon. He knew that he had what it took to do this, but Adriel was losing more than he was. So, Charles helped Adriel print everything out, and then Adriel remembered to get the information for Adeena and they headed back home.

Chapter 7
Complications Part I

While Adriel slept in the chair tossing and turning, there was a loud horn that sounded off outside their house. Arielle set up breathing heavily. She heard screeching tires in the drive away. She looked over at Adriel, but he hadn't budged. He opened one and peeped at her.

He said, "Don't worry. It has to be some drunken idiot playing games late at night. Go back to sleep."

She lay back down with her heart racing and turned over to her side. She didn't close her eyes as she was still rattled by it.

Arielle knew something was wrong, but she couldn't explain why she felt that way. She could feel her body tingling with energy. She heard someone walking fast in the hallway coming towards Adriel's door, so she turned over. It was Adeena, but she looked strange. Her hair was covering her face and her back was hunched over. Arielle became scared. She had never seen her sister like this before. Arielle screamed.

Adriel sat up feeling very agitated. He looked over at Arielle not noticing Adeena at first and was about to scold her for irritating him, but then he saw someone standing in the doorway. It was too late to respond. Adeena had made it over to him and pounced on him. She clawed at him and made horrible sounds. He tried to block every attempt she made to scratch him.

Arielle cried and jumped out of the bed. She ran up the hallway to get her father. She opened their door, yelled, and pointed towards Adriel's room which startled him. He ran down to Adriel's room and saw his son fighting off his sister.

Marcus pulled her off, but she seemed extremely heavy and strong for her size. Adeena was still clawing at the air and growling.

Marcus yelled, "Stop Adeena. Stop it now!"

She couldn't hear him. She was still in her trance. All she did was pierce at her brother in anger. When Marcus tried to hold her down, she tried to bite him. He would jerk his arm back. When he did that she would try to get away.

Marcus told Adriel to look for something to tie her down with. As soon as they got her in the chair, another horn sounded, but it was different from the first time. Adeena immediately slumped over. Marcus had to catch her before she fell. They sat her up. Cautiously they walked up to her hoping that she was asleep.

Adriel said, "Adeena? Are you there?"

She didn't move.

They quickly tied her to the chair before she woke up and something else happened.

Marcus went behind her and pulled her head up and saw her eyes were closed.

A few minutes later, Arielle came to the room and signed to her father saying that the doctor's car was at the end of the driveway when the horn went off again.

Marcus looked at Adriel and said," I knew it."

Adriel already had an idea that the doctor had hypnotized her. He didn't want to tell his father everything he knew because he dismissed him previously, so he kept everything he knew about the demon to himself. They untied Adeena from the chair and took her to her bedroom. Then tied her to the bedpost for the rest of the night, just in case the doctor decided to try it again.

Early the next morning, Adeena was screaming for someone to untie her from her bed. Adriel showed up laughing at her.

"Oh, you think this is funny, do you? Wait till I get out of this I will kick your butt," Adeena said angrily as she struggled.

Adriel explained to Adeena what happened overnight. Adeena immediately calmed down. Adriel untied her.

She asked him, "How often does this happen?"

"Not that often, last night, you clawed me like a cat," he smiled and showed her his arms. He continued, "I always knew you were feisty," he laughed.

She pushed him away from her jokingly, but it bothered her. She didn't like the fact that someone had used her for punishment against her family. She may have been jealous of her brother and little sister's relationship, but not enough to hurt him over it. She wondered if she had told this woman about that and she was using it against her to get revenge on him?

Adriel said, "We found out the name of what you call a shadow, it's Baymore. It isn't a shadow. It is a demon. Does that sound familiar to you?"

She sat there pondering over it for a few seconds.

Then as her memory came back, she leaned back on her bed and she started to think about everything.

Adeena told him that she did remember Baymore and that the demon would come to her at night only. It always would grab her and pull her to the closet. She never could understand why it did that. She would fight to get away from the demon.

As she was telling Adriel about what happened to her as a child, the room got cold. He noticed that Adeena had stopped talking. Adriel turned around to see why she stopped talking and was stunned by what he saw.

He yells, "Adeena! What's going on?"

Adeena was levitating into the air by something. He wasn't sure what was going on, but he knew something was there. Adeena was in severe pain as she was crying. Adriel called for his father.

Marcus came into the room and saw exactly what Adriel was seeing. Marcus tried to get to Adeena, but he was blocked by a forcefield. While Marcus and Adriel were trying to get to her, Adeena was listening to Baymore speak.

Baymore told her that if she didn't say the verse, then her little sister would eventually do what she could not. She had to make a choice. It would either be her or Arielle.

Baymore said, "Once you make a choice, I will no longer punish your sister. I will release your mother after I leave you today,"

Baymore tightened the grip on her throat and said, "You will have to make a choice soon."

She abruptly dropped back on her bed and the demon disappeared.

Adeena gasped for air as she held her throat. She couldn't look at her brother because she knew how much he loved Arielle. It would hurt her to tell him. Their father and Adriel hugged her. Marcus checked her body to see if she was okay. She had hand marks around her throat from where Baymore choked her.

She could barely talk.

Marcus said, "Don't say anything right now, let me get you some water."

Once their father left, Adriel asked her, "What happened?"

She looked at Adriel terrified and started to talk, but was interrupted. They heard their mother coming down the hallway holding onto the wall.

She yelled, "Marcus!"

Adriel looked up in amazement. Adeena was shocked as well.

Adeena knew Baymore had told her that he would leave her alone, but to see her walking was way more than she expected. She got up like the rest of them and went out to see her, but she stood behind everyone so that they all could show how overjoyed they were to see her up and moving. Her guilt started to eat away at her as she looked over at her little sister and her brother. She wanted so badly to tell them, but she knew the only way for them to be happy was to choose to be with Baymore.

Adriel looked back at Adeena and saw that she was in pain.

He said, "Let's get Adeena back into bed. She has been through enough for one morning."

Marcus said, "Yes, you're right."

Daniela said, "Hey it's my turn to be the caretaker," with a smile. Adeena smiled and got in the bed.

Later that day, Adriel went to Charles's house to get him so that they could go over the plans for trapping the demon. They headed to their favorite spot down by the creek. When they got there, Adriel told him about what happened that morning.

Charles was very baffled by what happened. He stated that he never gets to have anything like that happen in his house.

Adriel said, "You know Charles, you are one weird dude."

Charles laughed.

While they were talking about the demon, Charles kept looking back behind him.

Adriel was wondering why he did that.

He asked, "Is something wrong? Why do you keep doing that?"

Charles gave Adriel a shifty look.

He asked, "Doing what?"

Adriel responded, "You keep looking back. Do you hear or see something back there?"

Charles started playing in the dirt and got agitated. He then got up and started walking down the creek and tossed a rock. Adriel stood up waiting to hear what he had to say. He was worried that something was wrong as Charles seemed agitated.

Charles asked, "Did you guys ever find out what happened to Dexter?"

Adriel was perplexed by the question because he never told Charles he thought it was Adeena or anyone for that matter so he was wondering where this was coming from. Adriel said, "No, why?"

Charles turned around and he giggled. He looked at Adriel and said, "Well X Marks the Spot with a big smile."

Adriel's eyes had gotten really big. He was shocked, but then he started thinking. Adriel started to put the pieces together in his head. He was the one that originally called Adeena that. He was killing innocent animals with the slingshot. Adriel had been ignoring all the signs. He couldn't believe that he blamed his sister. Adriel started pacing up and down the creek. He began to get angry.

Charles was trying to explain to him why he did it, but Adriel couldn't hear him. He was doing his own logic in his head.

Adriel yells, "Just Shut Up! I understand that your father treats you and your stepmother like crap, but you could've left an innocent cat alone. That was my little sister's cat. You knew we would've been looking for it. You are my friend. This whole time we have been working on this, you never once thought to tell me anything. Now you want to bring this to me because we have to sacrifice something."

Adriel was questioning Charles's motive.

Charles walked over to him and said, "I am telling you because you can't do this part. You are not a killer. You won't tell your father the truth. Baymore was preying on both of our families. So, the one thing our family has in common is what?"

Adriel looked over at him shaking his head and threw his hands up. He ran up the path out of the woods and to his house. He left Charles by the creek by himself. Adriel didn't want to think about what Charles meant, but he knew exactly what he was thinking. Adriel was terrified about what Charles wanted to do. He was now scared of everything that came with this demon. He could see that both his sisters were suffering and he couldn't save them. He knew that he had to find another way to protect them. He had to do this on his own, without Charles.

Back home, Daniela came up with an idea for Adeena so that she wouldn't have to worry about hearing any more horns. She could use Arielle's iPod to listen to music and take them off as needed.

Adeena was a bit irritated by it, but she agreed. They tested it out while being tied up in a chair with their father going out to his truck and honking his horn. She had them on full blast and she couldn't hear anything, but it was too loud. They didn't want to take any chances. So they made adjustments to it so that she couldn't hear the horn. They made her keep it charged at all times and not take them off.

The next day, they took a trip to see Grandma Pearl, and Arielle wanted to use the iPod. Arielle was upset that Adeena told her no she couldn't have it. Adriel let Arielle use his. As the drive went on, they saw this sports car approach and Adriel leaned over to turn up the volume on Adeena's iPod. Adeena smacked away Adriel's hand.

She took her earpiece out and said, "You jerk, stop it."

He pointed to the car approaching and said, "Look."

She struggled to get the earpiece back in. The car got closer. Her mother urged her to hurry up, but she couldn't get it into her ear because she was so nervous. When the car passed, they saw it wasn't the doctor's car.

Adriel turned back from watching the car, he saw there was a car directly behind them. He grabbed the earpiece and stuck it in her ear. The person in the car behind them blasted their horn.

Marcus swerved the vehicle and slid in the gravel on the side of the road. The car sped off. As it did, their father saw the doctor smiling and waving. They all looked at Adeena, but she didn't react. Adriel had gotten the earpiece in her ear just in time. Adeena lent over and hugged Adriel. Adriel looked at his parents in relief.

They finally got back on the road to head to their grandmothers and when they got there, Adeena kept her headphones in.

Adeena walked over to her grandmother with a smile, hugged and kissed her on the cheek, which made her happy.

Grandma Pearl looked over to her daughter and said, "This is my Princesa."

Adeena went to sit in the corner chair so that she wouldn't be near a window and also to be near an outlet. Grandma Pearl noticed that she wasn't talking and it bothered her.

Adriel tried to distract Grandma Pearl from engaging with Adeena. He would do silly things and make her dance with him. It helped for a bit, but it didn't last very long.

Once Marcus and Daniela left the room, Grandma Pearl got up with her walker and went towards Adeena. She pulled out her earbuds.

Adeena was nervous, but she didn't panic. She didn't want her to know what was going on. She looked for Adriel to save her, but he was in the kitchen with Arielle so she smiled at her and said politely, "Yes Abuela?"

"Why is my little Princesa so quiet? I want to see you dance and sing like you used to. Is something the matter?"

Adeena said, "Oh nothing, I just really like listening to this music that's all."

She tried to put the earbuds back in, but Grandma Pearl felt offended and jerked them out of her hand.

She said, "While you are here, you will not be listening to that. I want you to be here with the family. You understand me?"

Adeena tried to reach for the iPod, but she put them in her rob and yelled for Adriel to come over.

Grandma Pearl turned to walk back, and as Adriel came out of the kitchen a loud horn sounded off. He turned and looked at Adeena and saw she didn't have her iPod. Adeena pushed Grandma Pearl and knocked her off her feet. Adriel closed the kitchen door. Marcus and Daniela came in after hearing the noise out in the hallway.

Daniela yells, "Madre!"

Daniela ran to her mother lying on the floor. She hit her head on the coffee table when Adeena pushed her. Marcus was trying to get Adeena to stop her from banging on the kitchen door and yelling. Daniela yells at Marcus to call the front desk for help. Marcus realizes how occupied he was and tells her that she has to go get help. He has his hands full with holding Adeena back.

When the ambulance arrived, the police were asking the parents questions. Adriel was looking around in the parking lot for the doctor's car. He didn't see it anywhere. Adeena was still screaming as they handcuffed her and put her in the back seat of the police car. Grandma Pearl was in the ambulance. They took to the hospital and Adriel and Arielle were sitting in the back of another ambulance being checked. Adriel knew his parents couldn't tell the police that a horn caused the disruption.

Adriel was so busy trying to find the doctor that he didn't realize the medical attendee was asking him questions. Adriel heard something vague in the distance and then a hand on his face. He shakes his head.

"Young man, can you hear me," the attendee stated.

"Oh sorry, what did you say," Adriel said in a daze.

The attendee repeated himself, "Did you or your sister ever get attacked during the altercation?"

Adriel calmly said, "No."

He turned his head and looked at Arielle and said, "She is just scared."

The attendee said, "Well I have checked both of you out and I see old scars on you son. I am hoping this is from an old accident, so I will let you go be with your parents."

Adriel looked up at him and gave a smile. He got up and took Arielle over to their parents.

The police officer was asking his parents, "Are you sure that your daughter isn't taking any medication that could cause her to act like this?"

Daniela said, "No officer, we are sure. Do you have to take her to the psych ward, Sir? Is it really necessary?"

She puts her head on Marcus's chest while he holds her.

Marcus asked the officer, "What do we need to do to keep this from happening."

The police officer replies, "Unfortunately, right now she can't be placed in a detention center. You said she isn't on anything, but she must have taken something. Until a doctor figures out what is wrong, she needs to be attended to by a specialist. You can come by in the morning tomorrow."

Daniela started to cry. The police officer gave them some paperwork and the phone number of the psyche ward. He got in the police car and drove off with Adeena in the back kicking and screaming.

Chapter 8
Complications Part II

Adriel was watching his parents bicker back and forth about what they were going to do about Adeena and not concentrating on how to fix the situation.

He snapped, "Would you quit it! None of this is going to fix it. Baymore is still going to take their souls, either way, you look at it!"

They were shocked but curious about what he meant. He knew he couldn't take it back after that. So, he told them only about the soul taking.

At that moment, the surgeon that had been working on Grandma Pearl had come out and called his parents over. The surgeon told them that she didn't make it through the procedure. Daniela fell to the floor whaling.

Arielle looked up at her brother and signed, "Did Baymore win?"

He said, "This time he did, little sis, this time."

Adriel was profusely upset. His mind wandered and he thought of what he had to do. He wasn't sure if he was going to sacrifice someone or thing, but he knew it wouldn't be anyone other than himself. He wasn't going to let Charles help him and he wasn't going to tell his parents. They would stop him and his sisters would suffer the consequences. He couldn't let anyone else die or suffer any further.

Back at the ward, Adeena was in a straitjacket. The nurses had to give her a second dose of medicine since she was not calming down. They didn't know what was wrong with her. They called the head doctor, but no response. The nurses called in a third male nurse to come and hold her down. The straps had broken loose. Once the male nurse came, Dr. Pavlovsky arrived and walked over to Adeena.

She grazed her hand across Adeena's head and said, "Don't worry, we will figure this out together."

She put her right hand in her pocket and pressed a button. A horn sounded off outside and Adeena calmed down immediately. She fell asleep as the medicine kicked into her system.

Dr. Pavlovsky ordered that Adeena did not have any visitors for at least a week. That way she could analyze her, draw blood work, and build a case study before she can be visited by anyone. The doctor went to her office and took out her file on the family. As she stopped to close her drawer, she pulled out an old photo of a child and an older man. It showed the older man smiling proudly with a fishing pole with small bait on the hook. The little girl standing on the other side of the fishing pole not smiling. She rubs the picture, flipped it over, placed it back in the drawer, and started on her notes.

The next morning, Daniela and Marcus went to see if they could talk to the head doctor about taking Adeena home. They were surprised to see that the head doctor was Dr. Pavlovsky. They knew immediately they would have complications. The nurse at the front counter didn't tell them that their daughter was on the no visitors list. She called Dr. Pavlovsky letting her know that they were there. Dr. Pavlovsky told the nurse to tell them that their daughter couldn't be seen today and they will have to wait until next week to see her.

The nurse responded with, "They aren't here to see her. They want to take her home and they have a note from the police officer at the scene that they can come today."

Dr. Pavlovsky hung the phone up and walked down the hallway to meet them.

She said, "I hear you have something for me."

Marcus said, "Yes, we were told we could see our daughter today by the officer that took her, but we came to get her. She isn't on any medication since we never started any treatment with you. So, we decided instead of leaving her here, we would like for her to come home. She is going through a lot and she is better off at home."

They looked at each other and Marcus handed her the form from the officer.

The doctor smiled and said, "Well this is just for visitation, not for removing her from this facility. Unfortunately, she attacked one of our staff members and we had to sedate her last night. She is still currently out and unfit for visiting. So, if you come back later or tomorrow, we will be more inclined to let you visit with her then."

Daniela stepped up to her and said in a low voice, "I am not stupid. We will be back here. You better not touch one piece of hair on my child's head. I know what you are up to, you and your little friend Baymore."

She looked the doctor in her eyes intensely and walked away as Marcus pulled at her arm.

The doctor smiled very evilly and said, "We will be here when you get back. Make sure you have the correct paperwork next time. Hopefully, she will cooperate with us and we won't have to sedate her again."

They went to the police station to talk to the officer that gave them the form. They noticed that there were only three officers on staff. Marcus went up to the clerk and asked for Officer Jefferson.

The clerk said, "Oh he went on vacation this morning with his family, can I get someone else to help you?"

Marcus looked at Daniela frustrated.

He said, "Well he helped us with our daughter's paperwork yesterday. She was sent over to the psych ward and he told us this form would help us get her out. We went there and now they are telling us that it is the wrong form. Is there anyone here that can help us?"

The clerk looked at the form and said, "We don't issue forms here to get your kids out of the ward. We only fill this form out to show they have been placed there so you can visit them. You have to go there to petition for them to be released after they have been analyzed. Didn't the doctor inform you about this when you were there?"

Daniela leaned on the counter.

She said, "That Ol' Battle Ax knew that and made us leave Marcus. I can't believe we fell for that. Our baby is stuck in that place with her. Damn it!"

Daniela asked the clerk, "Is there anything that you can do to help us get our daughter out of there?"

The clerk asked one of the officers to come over and help them. They gave the officer their information and the details of what happened at Grandma Pearls. He called Officer Jefferson. The officer let Marcus know that he will call them tomorrow when he has more information. They left and drove home unsatisfied.

Meanwhile, back at home, Adriel went to help Arielle with Peppa as she was still having a hard time walking from her injury. Since they are alone, Arielle used her telepathy and asked Adriel why he didn't play with Charles anymore.

Adriel shook his head and said to her, "I don't know. He is being a jerk and I am mad at him right now."

She thought about it and said, "Well Adeena was being mean to you and you forgave her, do you think you can forgive him? Did he do something that bad?"

Adriel thought about what she said and didn't respond. He just kept walking. When he realized he was walking by himself, he turned around and saw that Arielle and Peppa were still standing by themselves a ways back. He started walking towards her and called her name.

She didn't respond so he jogged back to her.

Adriel laughed and said, "Arielle, what are you standing here for?"

She pointed at the field beside them. She could see Baymore hovering in the field. Adriel couldn't see anything, but he believed her. He saw the fear in her eyes and Peppa was growling. The louder Peppa got, the closer Baymore got. Adriel picked Peppa up and he told Arielle to run to the house. She ran as fast as she could and Adriel stayed behind her because he remembered what happened to Adeena.

Peppa kept her eyes on Baymore and kept barking, as long as Peppa was barking Adriel knew Baymore was behind them. Arielle was at the foot of the steps and then all of a sudden, she fell. Adriel had sped up and put Peppa down. He turned to pick up Arielle and saw that she was hurt. She kept watching for Baymore. Peppa looked around and so did Arielle and they didn't see anything.

Adriel asked, "Do you see anything?"

She shook her head no.

Peppa limped in and Adriel closed the screen door. As he walked away from the door Baymore's eyes appeared in the doorway and Arielle screamed. She shut her eyes and buried them into Adriel's chest. Adriel closed the front door and locked it.

He asked, "Is Baymore gone?"

Arielle shrugged her shoulders and wouldn't look. He looked over at Peppa. She wasn't growling so he just took it as a sign that Baymore was gone.

When their parents came home, Adriel informed them that Baymore tried to harm Arielle while they were gone. While he was speaking, he realized Adeena wasn't with them when they got back. They shook their heads and thanked him for keeping her safe. He then asked where Adeena was?

His father said, "We weren't able to get her. Dr. Pavlovsky is the head doctor at the ward and she will keep her sedated until she behaves."

Adriel could tell that they were furious about this. His mother was pacing in the kitchen and his father was sitting at the table in a daze with his fist balled up. Adriel took Arielle to his room and told her to play with his game console for a while. He came back to the kitchen and asked his parents what they were going to do about Adeena? He knew that he needed to get his sister out of the ward. She wasn't crazy, but that the doctor was making her act like that. This demon and doctor had to go away, but how?

Daniela said, "That doctor has to go. We need to file a complaint of some kind."

Marcus said, "Right Daniela. I can see it now. This doctor is insane. She is consulting with demons and has placed my daughter in a hypnotic state. That will run well with the town. We will be hunted down and shot."

Daniela was frustrated and said, "Damn it, Marcus, what do you suggest. I don't want my daughter there with this crazy woman being experimented on and treated like a rag doll."

"Neither do I, but if we go in accusing her of witchcraft, she will rip us apart. We have to be smart about this," Marcus said.

Adriel was agreeing with his father on this, but in another way, he was thinking more like the crazy doctor. He needed a plan. How was he going to break her out of there? He needed to fix things with Charles and see if he could get Sasha to help as well.

So, he said to his parents, "I have a suggestion if your legit way of thinking doesn't work. Can we break her out? I mean Charles, Sasha, and myself? We did however get the information you needed about Dr. Pavlovsky without her knowing, right? I am sure we can find a way to get Adeena out?"

Daniela immediately shook her head no, but Marcus had a questionable look on his face. Daniela walked out of the room in disagreement. She was done with the conversation.

Marcus got up and patted Adriel on the back and walked into the living room where Daniela was.

He said, "Daniela, I think he has a good idea. Kids around here are barely noticed by people unless they do something wrong. I think that is why the doctor does this. Other adults don't pay attention to kids unless they make themselves noticeable. This town is not that big to begin with. Let's try what we can, and if it doesn't work, let them try. It won't hurt to hear what they come up with, okay?"

Daniela was not happy to hear anything that he had just said. He did, however, make a point that the doctor was playing off of the kids. So, she agreed to listen to their ideas. Adriel thanked them and he left out the door to head down to Charles.

Adriel wasn't ready to talk to Charles due to what he had told him about Dexter, but he knew he had to so that he could get his sister home. Once he got to his house, he heard things crashing and Charles's father yelling. He knew exactly what was going on. Charles was in the garage and he saw Adriel walking up to the house. He ran down to meet him.

"Hey Ads," he said with a sad face. "One day I won't be here to hear this mess anymore and he will regret that he ever lived to do that to anyone."

Adriel shook his head and they turned around to head towards Sasha's house. Adriel informed him about what happened to Adeena on the way to Sasha's house.

They arrived at Sasha's house and her parents had already heard about Adeena being taken by the cops. They told Adriel that she could no longer be associated with his family. That they were sorry and to never come back to their house. Adriel was shocked at their attitude and Charles spit at their door when they closed it.

Adriel laughed at him and said, "Dude what was that for?"

Charles looked back at the house and said, "They think they are better than everyone else, but they're not. I used to have a crush on Sasha, and I know you like her, but screw them."

Adriel looked up at Sasha's window. She closed her curtains as he looked up. He turned and they walked back to his house.

Adriel asked Charles what was the plan because he knew it was going to be tricky. This was harder than going into her office because her room is down a long hall that has nurses and doctors. It was like going into a hospital. They were going to need both Adriel's mother and father because they needed a lookout person to get by the receptionist and nurses. They will also need someone to get the keys, depending on if her room has a lock. When they go to visit the next time, they need to find out how they operate the place.

Adriel couldn't believe he thought this all out.

Charles said to him, "I watch a lot of investigative shows. I get in trouble so much, all I do is watch TV in my room," and he laughed.

Once they got back to the house, they went to the living room and Charles laid the plan out for his parents. They were amazed by what he said. Adriel smiled at Charles. He had almost forgotten that this was the guy that killed his little sister's cat for sport. This guy had just laid out a very detailed plan to break into the ward and get his sister out. He was doing something good for once. Was he trying to redeem himself for the bad he just did? Adriel was hoping this was a big change for Charles because he wanted to forgive him.

Daniela looked over at Adriel and said, "Well let's see what we can do on our part to get all the information that you need. If we can't do it, at least we can get everything that you need to get your end going. Oh My Gosh! We are officially criminals."

Daniela started laughing hysterically.

Marcus shook his head and told Charles, "I know we don't seem like the type of family that go around doing bad things like this. Please don't think of us like that. We love our daughter and she is going through a lot."

Charles interrupted him, "I already know about Baymore Mr. Gibson. You don't have to explain. Ads told me everything. Besides, that thing hangs out at my house on the regular with my father. I want to kill it myself."

Adriel grabbed Charles before he could tell them about what needed to be done. Charles was confused.

Adriel turned to his father and said, "Yes he knows and we will do what we have to, to make things right. Are we good?"

Marcus said, "Yes."

Adriel got up and ushered Charles to come outside with him so that he could walk him back home. As they headed back down the road, he informed Charles that he hadn't told his family about killing anyone.

Charles laughed and said, "I knew you couldn't get the nerve up to do that. One of us will have to. I will help you make this decision at some point. You know it's the only way."

Adriel didn't say anything, he just kept walking. Adriel then stopped in the street after realizing what he said.

He said, "I will call you when my parents have information that we need for getting my sister out. You know your way back home."

He turned around and started back home.
Charles yelled out to him, "You know I'm right Ads!"

Chapter 9
Prudent Planning

Daniela was extremely nervous approaching the front counter when walking into the psych ward that morning. She had already told her husband she didn't think it was going to work out. He had faith that it would, but it didn't give her much hope because something was nagging at her. She felt something about that day wasn't right. The officer had called and told them that the petition was denied. The only thing they could do was grant visitation as Adeena had already attacked the staff. The head doctor had petitioned for her to stay for two weeks for observation for potential treatment. Yet instead, Marcus was still in good spirits. They were going forward with Plan B, The Breakout. Which to Daniela meant jail time.

Daniela's head was spinning and she couldn't think. When they approached the nurse's desk her agony came to a halt. The same nurse from the other day was sitting there. She screened them in and the nurse handed Daniela a note in her hand as she wrapped the visitor's band around her wrist. Daniela thought it was a bit peculiar, but she didn't say anything. She crumpled the note in her hand and kept walking in the direction the nurse told them.

As they were walking, Marcus looked around for cameras and observed all the nurses' stations. He noticed that there were only two stations that were being attended. The other three were closed and no cameras were around them. They had windows with no bars on them. The nurse at the front desk had taken their phones from them so he couldn't take pictures. He was walking slowly to try to remember everything while he walked through.

When they got closer to Adeena's room, Dr. Pavlovsky approached them. Daniela bumped Marcus's arm to get him to stop looking around as they came to a halt. They allowed the doctor to come to them so they could keep their mind on what they were there for.

The doctor walked up to them and said, "I am glad you came today. Adeena is doing much better. She slept through the night and is no longer attacking anyone, but unfortunately, she isn't talking at the moment. We had an issue with her wanting to spit at the nurses when they tried to give her breakfast this morning. We had to muzzle her. However, she started to throw food on the wall. Now she is back in a straitjacket just in case she tries to attack you. This is just for precaution. We drew some blood to check to see what medications she may be on. Just in case she is on street drugs, you never know these days with these teenagers," as she laughed.

Daniela tried not to get angry because Dr. Pavlovsky knew that Adeena was fine.

Dr. Pavlovsky continued very snidely, "If she continues this behavior, we will have to move to drastic means and put her on medication. I am doing my best to refrain from doing that. I would suggest you talk to her and have her cooperate with us. Let us analyze her properly so that we can help her."

Marcus calmly asked, "So are you saying that we can't take her home at all today?"

Dr. Pavlovsky rested her hand on Marcus's shoulder and said, "I am so sorry Mr. Gibson. She isn't fit to leave the ward at this time. You are lucky to be able to see her right now with her behavior."

He looked down at her hand that was on his shoulder then back at her and he clenched his jaw. She immediately removed her hand. She ushered a male nurse to come and open the door to Adeena's room. Marcus saw the keys in the nurse's hand. They were not attached to anything. He watched him open the door and which key it was that he used to unlock the door. Unfortunately, he couldn't see where he went after he left the room as the door shut quickly behind them.

When they were in the room, Daniela had to get Marcus to focus back on spending time with Adeena. Marcus was more frustrated that the door closed too fast. When he turned around, he saw his daughter and didn't recognize her. Daniela put her hand over his mouth and hushed him as he was about to belt out a few choice words.

The muzzle on Adeena's mouth and the straightjacket had nothing to do with the fact that she had changed. Her eyes had sunken into her face and her hair had changed from medium brown to black and she looked frail. They knew something was wrong or that was not their child. Adeena got up and backed away into the corner of her bed. She was frightened to be around them. Every step they took to get near her, she would move towards the wall away from them.

Marcus was infuriated, which made him want to break her out even more. Marcus put his arm out in front of Daniela to stop her from moving any closer to her. Daniela's heart was broken seeing her that way. She turned around and began to cry. She grabbed her chest to calm herself down and remembered that the nurse had given her something. She looked around to see if there were any cameras in the room. She didn't see anything nor a window and she opened the note and told Marcus to look.

She wiped her eyes and read the note aloud in a whisper, "I have something to tell you about your daughter. Please meet me by the oak tree in the park at eleven fifteen. Dr. Pavlovsky can't be trusted."

Daniela looked at Marcus and she whispered, "What do you think?"

He shrugged and replied in a whisper, "We need all the help we can get," and looked back at Adeena.

He continued, "Look at our baby. She can't stay here. That woman is doing something to her."

Daniela said, "Well if we leave here calmly, she will know that we are up to something. I will keep crying and you just hold me as we walk out, but keep looking for the key."

Marcus nodded his head and they knocked on the door.

The nurse came to open the door while Daniela cried and Marcus held her. As he held her, Marcus talked to the nurse while the nurse was walking back to his station. He saw that he placed the keys on a rack. Daniela noticed that Dr. Pavlovsky was watching them as they were standing there. She kept crying and portraying being upset as long as she could, but the doctor didn't leave. So, she decided to become dramatic and stormed over to her and yelled at her to make it seem official.

She accused Dr. Pavlovsky of causing harm to her daughter. She told her to remove the muzzle from her face and stop treating her like an animal. Dr. Pavlovsky jumped and backed away from her. She wasn't expecting her to yell at her about the muzzle or being accused of anything. She was hoping for the way her daughter had changed. The attack took her by surprise. She turned and ran in the opposite direction. Daniela was relieved that she scared her, but it didn't give her any peace of mind about Adeena.

Daniela and Marcus went to the park and sat under the tree as requested by the nurse. She constantly kept checking the time on her phone.

Marcus rubbed her back and said, "Relax, it's only eleven ten, she will be here."

Marcus seemed as though he was calmer, but he was also nervous. He wasn't sure if they were being set up by Dr. Pavlovsky, but he didn't want his wife to know he was stressed out as much as she was.

He stopped rubbing her back as soon as he saw the nurse walking over and grabbed Daniela's hand.

He said, "Here she comes."

Daniela was about to get up and the nurse put her hand out to keep her from getting up. She walked on the other side of the bench to sit down with her lunch.

The nurse talked low so that only they could hear. "Please don't make this obvious. I sit here every day to eat lunch so that is why I chose this spot. Play on your phone, hold hands, do something that isn't obvious. I have been working here for about a year and I thought I had a great job, but one day I walked in on Dr. Pavlovksy's sessions with a patient and saw her hypnotizing them.

At first, I didn't think anything of it. Later, she came up to me and told me that I should never walk in on her sessions ever again. If the sign on her door showed that she was in session, then I should wait or come back later. She didn't have a sign on the door. I tried to tell her that, but she wrote me up for insubordination. The very next week that same patient was very ill and wasn't talking. They were muzzled for spitting at the nurses. After that, the doctor had another session with them. The patient was throwing things all over the room and attacking the staff. Dr. Pavlovsky was smiling and I had gotten a broken arm. They had to sedate the patient and the patient died the next morning."

The nurse took a bite of her sandwich and Daniela gasped.

Marcus looked up at the sky saying, "Lord help me."

The nurse finished chewing and then asked, "Did you see what she looked like in just a day? Tell me, is that normal for sedation? I don't know what she is doing when she hypnotizes them, but whatever she does, it isn't normal. You have to get her out of there. If you need my help, I am here."

Marcus turned slightly and said, "Well I think you were sent to us just in time. We were planning on doing just that. When do you work a night shift?"

The nurse scrolled through her phone and said, "I don't have one until this Saturday. She will be out of town, which makes that a great opportunity."

Daniela sat up and whispered to Marcus, "We don't know her, how can we trust her?"

Marcus whispered, "I know, but all we have is just us and we can't leave her in the hands of a psychopath either. She will die in there if we don't do anything. You saw what our baby looked like. That isn't our baby anymore. We already lost your mother. Do you want to lose her too?"

The nurse said, "You can trust me. Right after this, I am leaving town and getting away from this crazy place. I came here to get away from one psychopath and found myself in the hands of another. The last thing I want to do is stay around to be killed by this woman. By the way, my name is Sindy Hensworth. I know my name tag says Sin. They pick on me at work about my name. It was Dr. Pavlovksy's idea for using that nickname, and now I see why. She is pure evil. I will help you do whatever I can to get your daughter out of there."

Daniela was uneasy with the idea of her helping but Marcus gave Sindy his number and told her to call them when she got off of work. Sindy agreed. Marcus and Daniela left to go home.

Meanwhile, back home, Arielle had a visitor waiting for her in her room while she was eating lunch with her brother. Peppa didn't sense Baymore's presence this time and the demon made sure of it. Arielle slept and played in

Adriel's room now. Baymore had to find a way to lure Arielle away from her brother and Peppa. Arielle was heading up the stairs to go into Adriel's room, but she heard a noise coming out of her room. She went to her room to check it out.

Arielle walked to her door and looked in. She noticed that her lamp had fallen over so she picked it up. She took one last look around her room and then went for the door to walk out, but then the door closed before she could leave. Suddenly, a gust of air blew and knocked her down.

Adriel was downstairs washing dishes. He heard the door slam from in the kitchen and ran up the stairs. He knew immediately where it came from.

Arielle tried to get up but she was pinned to the floor. Arielle looked up and she saw Baymore hovering over top of her. She became frightened, but she knew what he wanted her to do and she didn't open her mouth. She heard her brother banging on the door.

Baymore said, "Say it or I will crush you." She felt Baymore pushing on her chest. Baymore looked up in the air as if someone was there.

Arielle looked up where Baymore was looking and didn't see anything there.

Baymore yells out, "No, not yet" and vanishes. The weight was lifted off of her. Arielle couldn't move because she was in so much pain.

Adriel came in and he saw his sister on the floor. Adriel sat Arielle up and she grabbed her chest. Adriel lifted her shirt and saw there were bruises on her chest. He called his father and told him what happened.

When their parents arrived, Marcus sat Arielle on his lap and asked her what happened. She tried to explain that Baymore wanted her to say the verse.

Her father was confused and asked her what she meant. She looked over at Adriel for help. Adriel walked off and started pacing in the kitchen. Their father repeated himself calmer because he didn't want her to get frustrated, but she shut down and they couldn't get her to tell him anything.

Adriel came back in and said, "I have the information that you need."

He went to his room and gave them everything that Charles and he had on Baymore.

Marcus and Danielle both were astonished about the information he had on the demon. They were also disappointed that Adriel and Charles were keeping it from them.

Daniela asked Adriel, "How do you think you were going to kill this demon? Who are you willing to sacrifice? You two aren't killers. You are just kids. What are you thinking?"

Marcus told her to calm down and said, "Look, I know you want to protect your sisters, but your mother is right. You two are just kids. Do you think that killing someone will justify anything? How do you know any of this will work?"

Adriel became defensive and said, "Have either of you been paying attention? This is not just a psychiatrist doing all of this. This is a freaking demon she is controlling. She is also trying to kill your kids and hurt people we love along the way. Charles's father is being controlled by this woman. Who is to say who else she is using this thing on?"

Marcus and Daniela just stood there and took in what he said. Adriel sat down at the table and put his head in his hands. He knew his parents understood the magnitude of the situation. He also knew there had to be extremes that needed to be done. He just didn't think they knew that killing the demon was the only answer. He started to believe that Charles was right.

That afternoon around three Marcus received a call from Sindy. He invited her to come over so that they could discuss in person what they were up against. She agreed and told them she would be by around seven that evening.

Adriel told his father to only tell her about the hypnotism and not the demon because he didn't want to scare her away. Daniela agreed, but Adriel needed to make sure that Charles didn't blow it. Adriel went to get Charles so that he was on board with the plan. When they came back, Charles wasn't as happy about Sindy not knowing. He felt that Sindy should know everything. Marcus told Charles she was only helping to get Adeena out, not helping with killing the demon. Charles finally agreed to be quiet and stuck with the plan.

Once Sindy arrived, Charles immediately became overwhelmed with infatuation. Daniela noticed it as soon as Sindy started walking up to the door. Charles went to open the front door as Sindy approached. Daniela giggled. Marcus was confused about what was going on. He looked at Adriel then back at Daniela. He saw Charles was using his manners. He introduced himself, which was very odd. Sindy didn't pay him any attention and she walked in ignoring him.

Charles sat down and stared at Sindy while they were going over the plan and all he said was, "That sounds cool to me."

Adriel couldn't believe what Charles had agreed to. He pulled Charles to the kitchen, snapped his fingers in his face

He said, "Loverboy, wake up. This is serious. You are not paying attention. My father is asking you to climb in a window to steal the key and you said that sounds good to me."

Charles' eyes widened.

He replied, "Wait! What! I didn't agree to that. I thought you were the sneaky one. I can only talk to people and distract them. I can't do that."

Adriel shook his head and pushed him back into the living room.

He said, "Then snap out of it and pay attention."

Adriel stopped his father and told him their plan.

Marcus was surprised that they had a plan. Daniela wasn't surprised, since they had hidden information from them originally.

Sindy smiled and was very pleased with the information they had and said, "This sounds promising."

Marcus told Sindy to be ready and when Charles showed up to make sure she left her station as planned.

Sindy said, "Oh, by the way, I have something for you guys." She gave them a copy of the key to Adeena's room.

Daniela looked at Marcus.

Marcus said, "You know this will get you caught or in jail?"

Sindy smiled and said, "We all have spare keys in our drawer and this one belongs to a girl that was fired three months ago. They changed her keys out already. I just so happened to check and it fits Adeena's door. I matched it up the other day when I took Adeena her lunch."

Charles looked over at Adriel and saw that he didn't like that she had the key. He looked over at Daniela and she had the same face.

Charles grabbed the key out of Sindy's hand and said, "That was very nice that you are sacrificing your job to help. We appreciate everything that you are doing to help us with this. I can't wait to see you Saturday," and he gave her a hug with a smile on his face.

Sindy felt awkward. He patted him on the back and waited for him to let go.

Daniela got up and escorted Sindy to the door.

Daniela said, "Thank you for coming tonight, we have so much to think about as Saturday is several days off from now. Can you please give us updates on her?"

Sindy turned to her and gave her a stern look.

She replied, "I have no problem doing that. I hate what they are doing there and I don't trust her. I am only doing this because I want to help you. I am leaving directly after this is over. I suggest you do the same. I will give you daily updates if that is ok with you?"

Daniela nodded and thanked her again. Charles ran to the door to get out so he could walk Sindy to her car.

Adriel shook his head and then walked over at his father

He asked him," What do you think?"

Marcus said, "He is a complete moron."

Adriel laughed and then he said, "No, about Sindy and the plan?"

His father sat back and said, "Well son, part of me wants to believe she is telling the truth and the other part thinks somehow she is a smokescreen. We won't know until something happens. We just have to play it out. Personally, if we don't use this key, we need to get the key just like we planned from the nurses' station. That part stays the same."

Charles came back with a smile on his face. They all looked at him like he was a complete idiot.

Chapter 10
The Breakout

Saturday was here and Adriel hasn't slept a wink. His mind was twirling and his nerves on edge. He wasn't eager to do the impossible task of the ultimate sacrifice, but this break out was exhilarating for some reason. He started to wonder if this was how Charles felt about killing animals with the slingshot. He decided to listen to his iPod and try to tone out his thoughts. He began to have the image of his dream paying in his mind of his sister with blood on her face from his dream. The excitement seems to drift away.

Meanwhile, Daniela was already downstairs cooking breakfast her emotions were quite the opposite. Cooking and cleaning was a coping mechanism for her. Her nerves were on edge because she felt like it was going to be a disaster and they were going to get caught. She had cooked more than the usual breakfast and no one seemed to notice.

While Daniela was fixing breakfast trying not to overload the stove, Marcus came to the room to check on Arielle and Adriel. Adriel told him that Arielle had nightmares again. The demon didn't come this time, but he held her the whole night to help with her nightmares. He didn't know if that had anything to do with it, but he knew that with him being around, it did have an affect on things. His father reassured him that his mother will watch her in the truck while they are working tonight and that she will be okay.

There was a knock at the door.

Marcus turned to Adriel and asked, "Charles isn't coming later right?"

Adriel replied, "I thought so."

They both left out the room to go see who was at the door as Daniela was already there.

Daniela opened the door and saw it was Dr. Pavlovsky.

Marcus came around the corner and he yelled, "What do you want now woman?"

"I didn't mean to intrude; I just wanted to tell you that I will be leaving this weekend for some time to myself. We are closed on weekends and I didn't want you to burden yourself to come out to visit your daughter. I just wanted to stop by with an update to let you know we are making great progress with her. She has stopped making aggressive actions against my staff and we have taken the muzzle off of her. She still hasn't spoken yet, but she is calm now."

Daniela walked away from the door and Marcus stepped to the door to keep her from trying to enter the house.

He placed his arm in the doorway and said, "Anything else?"

She smiled, then said, "As long as she stays silent, we will have to keep her at the institution. I am afraid she will be there for a while. We are seeing progress in her aggression. However, we are not progressing with an answer on why she has killed your mother-in-law. Until then, you will not get your daughter back."

She smiled at him, waved goodbye, and turned to walk down the front stairs towards her car.

She yelled back, "I will be back on Monday. If you have any questions, please feel free to call my staff over the weekend or call me on Monday. I hope we can come up with a great plan. Have a good weekend."

She waved to them as she got in her car.

She backed her car out the driveway and sped down the road.

Marcus slammed the door and said, "Oh we are definitely getting her out now."

Daniela slammed her fist into the wall, which made Peppa bark and scared Arielle.

Adriel came into the room and asked, "Now you understand why we need to get this done tonight?"

Daniela nodded her head while she was still pacing.

As the day went on, they all went their separate ways to get themselves focused until Sindy showed up. Charles was sitting on the front porch waiting for her to arrive. He ran over to her car. For some odd reason, he wouldn't let her get out of her car. He made a fool of himself tripping over his own feet to get there. Adriel walked away from the door as Charles talked Sindy to death by her car. Adriel couldn't hear what they were talking about, but he saw that she was confused. She nodded her head. He finally opened the door and she got out of the car.

During the discussion, Sindy informed them that she needed to be at work by eleven and it was currently nine. Charles informed them that he was going to be the distraction and Sindy was going to make sure a side window was open for them to get in. Sindy told them that the cameras were already adjusted so that no one would be able to view Marcus and Adriel as they entered the building. Sindy would make her rounds distracting the male nurse that was sitting at Adeena's station.

They all agreed that this was the plan, even though Marcus knew he was still going to steal the key at the station. He still felt that Sindy giving them this key was a bit too easy. Daniela and Arielle would remain in the truck listening on the cell phone that Charles had in his pocket while he monitored the cameras in case of an emergency. Sindy would angle her monitor towards Charles when she got up. If anything happened, he would use the safe word "Pumpernickel" so that Daniela would know they were aborting the mission.

Daniela didn't understand how that would be used delicately, but Adriel assured his mother that Charles had done it before. Sindy and Marcus both laughed at this idea, but once the meeting was over Sindy left to go to work.

The kids played outside for about an hour and then Marcus called them to get in the truck so they could head out. It was around twelve by the time they would get there. Sindy had sent a message to Marcus with the go-ahead. The night was full of stars and Arielle wanted to sit on the back of the truck and listen to her iPod. Daniela told her to be careful, so they had Peppa sit back there with her. Adriel turned around in the back seat to watch her.

Charles noticed that Adriel was very protective of his siblings. He doesn't have any, but he admires that in Adriel. He understood exactly why his father didn't like Adriel.

He said, "For some reason, my father doesn't like you. I'm thinking it's because you're a good person. Baymore may have something to do with it though. If the demon never existed, none of this would have happened. I am going to put a stop to all of this. You won't ever have to go through any of it again. I promise."

Charles stopped watching his sister for a moment. He took in what Charles had said. He knew that Charles cared a lot about his family and he was also suffering, but it scared him to know that Charles would to great lengths to protect him. What did he have planned? He turned and looked out the side window.

Marcus heard what Charles said, but he didn't want to say anything. He knew that Charles' father was a bitter man. The whole town heard about what he does to him and his stepmother. He saw the concern on his son's face and wondered what Adriel was thinking. He just looked at the both of them in the rear-view mirror and kept driving.

They approached the parking lot a little after twelve and Marcus texted Sindy to let her know they were there.

Daniela called Charles's phone and they all put their phones on silent to make sure nothing would get interrupted. Sindy told them they were good to go. They all looked at each other and said good luck.

Arielle and Peppa came inside the truck while Charles went to the door and rang the bell. As he stood there, Marcus and Adriel ran to the open window on the side of the building where there was a ladder. Marcus angled the ladder on the wall and waited for the second message from Sindy. They didn't know that Charles hadn't entered the building yet.

Daniela saw that Charles was still at the door. Her leg shook in the truck and she started muttering to herself, "What is going on? Why isn't anyone coming to the door?"

Charles rang the bell for the third time. He began to bang on the door. He cupped his hands on the window to look inside. Finally, he saw someone coming to the door.

A man in a dark uniform opened the door and told him to back up.

The man said, "May I help you?"

Charles smiled and replied, "Why yes! I was told that I was supposed to come here tonight to help with cleaning the building for an internship. I have been waiting here ringing the bell and no one opened the door. I am severely late. Please tell me this isn't how it's going to be every night?"

The man gave a snarl at him and motioned for him to come in. Within a minute Marcus got a text for Sindy to proceed.

As Charles entered the building, he looked around and noticed that there weren't that many people in the building. The lights were very dim and he walked directly to the front desk where Sindy and another lady were. The man, who seemed to be a security guard, was only carrying a nightstick and a flashlight. The security guard walked away and didn't say anything to the women about why Charles was there. Charles realized he could have told a completely different story altogether if he wanted to, but he had to stick with that story because Sindy had put him down for an internship.

Sindy and Charles didn't make eye contact when he approached. He looked directly at the nurse in front of him to make sure she got his undivided attention so that she didn't see anything that Sindy was doing. Once she started to talk to Charles, he messed around with everything on her desk and caused the distraction. Sindy turned her monitor in his direction.

He made random jokes to make her laugh and she forgot why he was there. She never started his paperwork. He then picked up several of her pins as they were talking to make her eventually pick them up later once everyone was on the verge of leaving.

When Sindy was done doing her setup, she stopped Charles talking by saying politely, "Excuse me, I'm about to do my rounds. It looks like you can handle this from here. I will be right back, okay?"

The other nurse smiled and brushed her off. Sindy chuckled and walked off.

Meanwhile, Marcus opened the window and poked his head through to make sure there wasn't anyone in the area and that no cameras were focused on the window. He climbed through. Once he got in, he then peeked around the corner and went back to the window. He ushered Adriel to come in. As soon as Adriel got in, they both turned around and Sindy was there. It took everything in their power not to scream.

Marcus grabbed her and said, "What the heck is your problem woman?"

She didn't realize they had just come in the window. She had just gotten over there at the same time.

She said, "Sorry, I just started on my rounds and saw you as I came around the corner. I'm sorry. I will head over to get them out of the building now. Just wait five minutes so I can get him outside."

Adriel leaned against the wall catching his breath and he looked at his father laughing.

Marcus said, "I think she is going to screw us. You see how she was here when we came around the corner."

Adriel said, "I think you're paranoid, she seemed very sincere, so just calm down. Give her five minutes as she said. We are just anxious to get Adeena out of here, that's all."

Marcus was doubtful, but he waited as she asked.

Five minutes seemed like an hour and while they waited, a swarm of thoughts was going through his mind as to what she could be up to.

Unfortunately, the same thing was happening with Daniela. Daniela was getting irritated by the conversations that were taking place with Charles. She felt his demeaning characterization of women was pathetic. She knew he was playing a character, but this woman was stupid to fall for a twelve-year-old kid. She felt he sounded like a grown man hitting on a woman and she was falling for every little line he was throwing at her. She wanted to come through the phone and smack him. She kept saying in her head to hurry up Marcus, but she knew it would take some time.

While they were waiting, they looked around to make sure no one was watching them. Even though it was a small town, she knew that the people there were well-knitted. She started to become overly paranoid. She was hoping that Sindy didn't lie to them and the security guard wasn't going to show up and arrest them for breaking in to get Adeena out.

Back inside, Sindy approached the nurses' desk. She asked the male nurse if he would like to take a break with her and have a quick smoke break before he made his rounds.

He smiled and said, "Sure, might as well. Nothing is happening at this time of the night anyway."

He got up, placed his keys on the rack, and walked away with her. They went out to the break area and he put a brick in front of the door to keep the door from locking them out. He watched her while she lit her cigarette.

He asked, "Can I ask you a question?"

She blew some smoke from her mouth and said "Sure."

He leaned forward and whispered, "How come we never hung out? We take smoke breaks together. You never go out with any of the people here or eat lunch with anyone here, but you take a smoke break with me all the time. Why is that?"

She looked over at him and said, "Well we are the only ones that work the late shift together that smoke and it's boring to smoke alone. It's just that simple."

He laughed and said, "Well yeah, it has been very boring smoking alone until you got here."

She changed the subject to divert him away from the obvious. She didn't want him to realize what was happening at the moment. They started talking about work and television shows to pass the time.

Back inside, Adriel and Marcus went down the hallway to the nurses' station to get the key. When they got there, Adriel noticed the camera was on the nurses' station. Adriel stopped his father and pointed to the camera. Marcus was startled by this. Adriel told him to use the key that Sindy gave them. Marcus had no choice but to try. He felt deep down inside it was the wrong key, but he went ahead and got the key out of his pocket and stuck it in the hole. He took a deep breath and turned the key.

The key fit. He looked back at Adriel and smiled in amazement. He opened the door to Adeena's room, but he didn't see her. Marcus entered her room, went over to her bed, and flipped over her matters thinking she was under her bed. He forgot that the door closes behind him and he had taken the key with him in the room. The door closed with Adriel outside of the door. Adeena was behind the door as it opened, closing him inside the room with her and her father locked in the room together.

Adriel was shocked when the door closed. Not knowing what to do. His father was locked in the room with his sister and the camera could show him getting the other key. He didn't know how much time he had left before Sindy could come back with the other nurse or if anyone else could come down the hall.

All he could hear was his father saying to Adeena, "I am your father Adeena, we came to get you. We are going to take you home. I love you."

Adriel began to panic. He then realized that if he could turn the camera in another direction, he could go and get the key. He looked around for something to angle the camera in another direction so he could go over and get the key. Adriel got a stool then stood on it and turned the camera towards the wall.

Charles saw what was going on and tried not to respond.

He said randomly during the conversation with the nurse, "There are unforeseen things, that are happening right now that can't be changed. That should be changed and will need to be changed. It's just like life."

He ranted on in code with the nurse to get Daniela to understand what he meant. Daniela was confused by his ranting. She realized what he said had nothing to do with his conversation with the nurse. She was just as lost as the nurse until he repeated it twice. She then realized something went wrong and he didn't use the safe word which made her worried. Daniela started to grip the steering wheel tightly and pleaded under her breathe for them to hurry up. She looked over at Arielle and saw that she wasn't worried.

Arielle smiled at her mother and signed to her, "Everything is going to work out. I promise."

Meanwhile, Adriel decided to move the camera. He got the key from the station and opened the door. He made sure he found something to hold the door open so she couldn't lock them both in. He saw her growling and foaming at the mouth. Her hair was black and she was pale. She was on all fours in a position ready to attack their father.

He firmly spoke to Adeena, "Adeena stop!"

She immediately stopped trying to scare their father and turned to him.

Adriel then said, "Stop this right now. Come with me if you want to get out of here?"

She stood up and grabbed his hand. She followed him out towards the hallway. They closed the door and led her to the window. Adriel let their father go first.

Adriel explained, "You will have to climb down. Do not hurt our father or make any noises. Understand?"

She nodded her head, climbed down, and ran to the truck.

Daniela hung the phone up and texted Charles that they were in the truck. When Daniela saw her daughter running beside Adriel, she was happy at first. Then as she got closer, her heart plummeted. Adeena looked over at her with the blackest eyes she had ever seen. Daniela hadn't felt so much hate and coldness forced upon her since she, herself was younger. At that moment she felt hopeless. When Marcus got in the passenger seat and told Daniela to start the truck, he saw that Daniela was frightened. He hadn't seen her like that in years. He told her to move over to the other side and he will drive back.

Adriel sat in the bed of the truck with Adeena to keep her away from everyone else. A few minutes later, Charles came out. He had a smile on his face and he was pumping his fist in the air. He wanted to sit on the back of the truck with Adriel and Adeena, but Marcus stopped him before he did. On the way back he watched them the whole back while they were sitting back there.

Marcus kept looking in the rear-view mirror at Adriel and Adeena. He was so confused at how his son could get her under control. He then remembered what Charles had said to Adriel on the way there. He looked back at Charles and saw how he was watching them. He was afraid of what the outcome would be of this situation. What did he mean by the one thing you love the most? Does it have to be Adriel or Charles? He then looked over at Arielle who was sleeping with her iPod on. He grabbed his wife's hand and pondered intensely about what was going on in Charles's mind and why his wife was so shaken up.

Chapter 11
Dr. Pavlovsky

A young girl by the name of Lauren Pavlovsky grew up in a small town in Germany with her father. She was a shy and distant child because she lost her mother at a young age. Her father, however, was a very loving and cheerful man who enjoyed many outdoor adventures such as fishing and hunting in which he took her along with him. Being that these activities were male-oriented, it was shunned upon by most to see a female engaging in them. He didn't care as his daughter was everything to him and he knew she loved it even though she never showed it with emotions. He knew by when she drew him pictures of their adventures and she would run to him with her fishing pole.

One day, there was a family gathering. A woman she had never seen before was watching her. She could tell her father was very uncomfortable about it. He told his brother to have her removed from the house. Lauren asked her father who the woman was and why did he have her removed? He told her to not worry about it. She was of no concern to her.

The next day he took her fishing and they had pictures taken by the pond where they were fishing.

He asked his daughter, "Why do you not smile anymore my dear."

She said, "What is the point of showing anyone that side of me for them to take it away?"

Her father replied, "They can't take anything away that you never gave them, to begin with."

She was confused by his statement.

She said, "Who took my mother away from me?"

She walked away from him without giving him a chance to respond. Her father stood by the pond baffled by her question and full of remorse. He loved his daughter. He raised her to be proud and strong. He never thought she would be angry about her mother's death.

The very next morning she woke up to bring her father breakfast. She found her father dead in his bed. She was informed that he died from a heart attack. Lauren didn't cry, she didn't grieve, nor did she become angry. She went to her room, sat on her bed, and read a book. She became numb to her emotions.

At the funeral, her uncle told her she would be living with a woman that will help her understand her place in history and will be teaching her how to be a lady. She would be moving to America. He told her she didn't have any relatives left in Germany that could take her in as he was too old to take care of her and they couldn't afford to. This caused Lauren to become angry.

When her uncle brought her to the home of the woman and introduced Lauren to her, she saw it was the same woman that her father had kicked out of the house. She backed away from her uncle and ran down the driveway towards the street. Before she could enter the street, the gates closed automatically. There was no way for her to climb the gates.

Her uncle walked down to talk to her and said, "She isn't a bad person. Your father doesn't want you with her because she is your mother's aunt and she is from America. When he found out that your mother was an American, he cut her off from her family and told her to never speak of it to anyone, especially you. Your mother faked being

German for a very long time. He hates Americans and that's why he didn't want her around. Please give this a try. You deserve to be happy."

She didn't know whether to believe him or not, but she didn't have anywhere to go.

She walked back to the house and saw that the house was old and it smelled funny. She looked around and noticed that the furniture wasn't old, but the place was old. Lauren approached the woman. She was of average height with young features. She didn't seem to be old at all. She thought to herself, how was she her mother's aunt? She didn't know how old her mother was, so maybe that could explain it.

The woman spoke and said, "Lauren, I am Karen Lotts. I am your great aunt. You can just call me Karen. You will be staying with me here for a few days as we need to hash out the details with the lawyers. Then we will go to America to my place in Kansas. Your mother already had your passport and granted you dual citizenship when you were born so I don't have anything to do other than the legal paperwork for your guardianship. Unfortunately, your father has been giving me a hard time introducing us since your mother died sweetheart. I am very sorry for that. I will do my best not to frustrate you. I will let you relax. When you are ready to talk to me, I am here."

Lauren just looked at her. She thought she was weird being that her accent was strange. She had heard Americans speak before, but she had never heard one with an accent like hers. She also didn't want to believe that her mother was an American. She had heard her mother speak English and she never sounded like that before. Her mother was German and she didn't trust this woman.

Her uncle walked off with Karen talking. Lauren looked around at the pictures on the walls in the Fourier. She saw pictures of her mother and Karen with other people together as a group like a family portrait. She looked back at Karen thinking she played a prank on her. She knew there was no way that her father couldn't have told her about these people. She would have at some point seen something in her house. Then she saw an old fashion picture of a little girl that looked just like her, but with light brown hair. Then another girl and a boy, but with the same parents and a dog. She looked back at the other pictures and was confused because they looked like they were in different timelines.

Lauren took out her picture of her and her father. She looked up at the pictures and was baffled at the resemblance between her and her mother. Her mother looks just like her but with brown hair. She ran out on the front porch and cried. She couldn't believe it was true.

Her uncle came to the door. He asked if she wanted to talk, but she didn't answer. He went back to get Karen. She came out and she sat beside her.

She saw the picture and said, "Your mother was a beauty. She was intelligent and adventurous. I hope that we can make something great out of our time together. It's getting dark. Let me show you to your room so you can get settled in."

As time went on, they moved to Kansas and Lauren didn't see what the big deal was about living in America. She hated being away from her father's home. She began to hate Americans and the kids she grew up with. She felt they were acting as if they were entitled to things. Karen bought her beautiful things to make her feel and look pretty, but it only made her feel worse. Her daughter tried to help her make Lauren feel welcomed, but eventually, even she distanced herself from her. Lauren constantly shuts herself off from other people and the household. Karen knew she had to do something about it as she was getting older and it was getting out of hand.

Karen noticed that Lauren was very shut off emotionally. Lauren learned about American cultures, emotions, and antics. She needed her to fit in with the general population to not seem too different. She couldn't change her accent, but she could change her presentation when being around people. Lauren fought hard with her about changing her personality being she couldn't stand being there. She agreed that when she was around people, she would pretend to be happy or at least, aware of her surroundings.

As Lauren got older, closer to high school graduation, Karen told her she wanted to show her something that would give her answers to what she thought would put to rest her suspicion of what happened to her mother. Karen took her to the basement. She opened the door to what Lauren originally thought was the wine cellar. She saw it was filled with candles and witchery items. Lauren slowly walked in and stopped midway and waited for Karen to explain herself. Karen told her to step forward and look at a book she had at the podium.

Lauren slowly walked over. She looked and it was in German, which she wasn't expecting. She started reading and saw it was about a demon named Baymore. Karen told her that Lauren's father had cursed her mother with the demon because he thought she was cheating on him with another man. He wanted to make her go mad, but instead, the demon didn't make her go mad, it made her ill and then eventually it killed her.

Her father didn't do the ritual correctly and it backfired on him. Eventually, it took his life when it came to him that evening after they went fishing. She explained to her that was why he took the photo, so she could have something to remember him by. He knew he was going to die.

Lauren didn't believe her. She shoved the podium and it fell over as she ran out of the room.

The next morning, she didn't come out for school so Karen came to her door. She pushed three letters under her door. The letters were addressed from Lauren's mother to Karen. She read each one. The first two were about how she wanted to get away from her husband that was abusing her and keeping her hostage. How she could only see her beautiful child once a week if she would behave herself. She needed help to get away. He only allows her to eat one meal a day and it was making her sick. She wanted to take her daughter and leave. A man was helping her, but he was afraid that if he kept talking to her, her husband may take it the wrong way

. Lauren started to cry. She remembered seeing her mother sick in the bed as a child, but she couldn't remember anything before that. She tried to remember playing with her or doing anything other than seeing her in bed. It was upsetting to her that this was becoming true that her father was a cruel person.

She opened the last letter. She noticed in this letter it stated that it was going to be the last one. It read, "*Enclosed is Lauren's passport, birth certificate, social security card, and my Will. I know he is trying to kill me. Please take care of her. I don't know what is going on, but the gentleman that is sending these letters to you will make sure she will get to you safely. Please do not let his family raise her. Teach her our ways well and keep her safe. Let her know I love her. She is neither good nor bad.*"

Lauren stopped reading after that and fell on her bed crying. Her mother was killed by her father and then he died by his own hand. Karen was telling the truth. She couldn't believe it. She didn't know why it was happening to her. She wasn't angry or sad, but she knew now that both of her parents were killed by a demon. She knew she had to learn more about this demon. Karen told her that her father didn't control it and that was why it killed him.

She put the letters back in the envelopes and placed them under her mattress. She gathered herself and went down to the kitchen.

She said to Karen, "Teach me how to control it."

Chapter 12
Control Issues

As Lauren drove to her great aunts to get assistance on why she lost control of Baymore. She started looking over at the box, thinking back to when she was younger reading her mother's letters. She knew that if she didn't get this demon under control she would eventually die. She didn't know how many people the demon had already killed, but she knew that Adeena was turning. She couldn't let her die like the previous child. She pulled into the driveway and saw Karen standing on the porch. She looked as young as she did when Lauren was a teenager.

She brought the box and the book to Karen and said, "I am losing my grip on the demon. It got away from me and was after the little one without me knowing. The other child is turning into death itself. I didn't request the demon to do anything and it was torturing her without my asking. How can this be?"

Karen had her go to the basement. They went to the podium and opened the book. They placed materials on the floor and looked through the information.

Karen said, "You have someone there that is too close to the light. That is what is interfering with your agenda, and the demon is trying to take both of them from that person. If Baymore finds them as a threat, you know the demon will want to make them suffer. Your connection with

Baymore is gone, my dear. You have no sway over that demon anymore."

Lauren became infuriated and started pacing in the room. She knew exactly who Karen was talking about.

She mumbled to herself saying, "That little rat. I knew this would happen. I should've killed him myself."

She asked Karen how she could get Baymore to obey her again. Karen told her it couldn't happen unless they banished the demon and resurrected it all over again. They would have to wait five years for the bones to rest.

Lauren bit her nails, then looked over at the book.

She said, "Is there another way to cause pain on the boy?"

Karen was concerned and closed the book.

She said, "My dear child, what has this child done to you that you need to inflict pain on him so badly?"

Lauren's eyes were bloodshot red and she became crazed with anger.

She said, "I have one of his sisters at my ward. His little sister is very special. He will do anything to protect his family, but I had no plans on killing them. I just wanted to see how far he would go to protect them. The one in the ward could see the demon and she was the one that should have been turned in the first place. I honestly don't care about her anymore. She can suffer the way I left her. Her brain is mush," and she laughed hysterically.

She further said, "Her family will never have her back the way she was. She will never love them or care about anyone else ever again."

Karen asked, "What did you do to that girl?"

Lauren flopped down in a chair, "I made her feel and see all the bad things in the world. I had the demon put images in her head. I gave her all the memories from the kids and people that the demon had tortured, including my parents. It changed her mentally and physically. Her mind is no longer hers. Once I send her back to her family, they will never love her the same. You see, Baymore did exactly what I have always wanted him to do. I didn't want him to kill for me. I just wanted him to inflict the pain that I have been feeling my whole life on someone else. Now someone else will feel the way I feel."

Karen was ashamed of what Lauren turned into. She felt sorry for Adeena. She asked Lauren whose daughter it was and Lauren told her.

Lauren said, "It's too late. I know you will do what you can to help her so don't. I have looked through the book and there isn't a way to reverse it. Her mind is destroyed. She could never forget what she has seen. I made sure of that."

Karen patted Lauren on the shoulder and walked back up the stairs to the kitchen to put tea on for them.

While she was making the tea, she began chanting an incantation in her mind to bind Baymore back to his dimension.

Lauren came up the stairs and asked for a cup.

Lauren said, "Is there anything that you could teach me that may help me control him from doing anything else? I wasn't able to call him just a second ago to have him go check on Adeena."

Karen replied, "I told you he isn't connected to you anymore. It sounds to me that he had completely disconnected from you. If I were you, I would destroy his bones and put him under so he doesn't kill anyone. I can help you with that if you need me to."

Karen remained calm to keep her from suspecting anything. She didn't want Lauren to know that she had bound the demon from being able to do anything further.

Lauren sat at the table, blew into her tea, and took a few sips. She sat back in her chair. Karen saw she was getting sleepy and didn't say anything. Karen never drank any of her tea, she just held the cup in her hands.

She then got up and said, "I am going to take a nap and then figure out what to do."

She left the tea on the table. Lauren had put an elixir in her cup before she had come up to make her sleepy.

Lauren went back downstairs to get her stuff and took them to her old room. Lauren wasn't sure why her great aunt wanted to get rid of the demon, but she wanted to know why it had disconnected from her. She tried to think back to when everything disconnected. She looked over her notes on Adeena, then over her notes from when she wrote about Adriel and Arielle. She realized she had seen where the demon may have encountered other people in the town without her knowing. She didn't know how this could have happened.

As she reviewed, she saw a notation where all three people talked about one person in common, Charles. She couldn't figure out why this boy was important. She went years back and saw an old note from a previous patient, which was a woman that just had a baby boy. She was arrested at a bar for being drunk in public. When the police officer arrested her, she spits at him and was accusing the officer of abusing her. They found fresh marks on her body, but the officer hadn't touched her. They figured that she made the marks herself because she was drunk and maybe she had fallen or run into something.

Once she had gotten to the ward, Lauren uses her as part of the demon's experiment. This woman just had Charles a few months ago and Lauren never put the pieces together until now. She still didn't understand why Charles was important. Somehow, she felt Charles was the key. She started to feel dizzy. She placed everything aside and went to sleep.

When Karen sensed that Lauren had fallen asleep, she began calling to find information on Adeena. She called Lauren's ward and the person that answered the phone was Sindy. Sindy asked why was she asking about Adeena Gibson and who she was. Karen told her that she was a concerned party and that she would like to get in touch with her family to help with her situation. She knew that Ms. Pavlovsky was out for the weekend and will be back Monday. She didn't have a lot of time and it was urgent. To please have them get in touch with her as soon as possible. Sindy was shocked and didn't know what to think about it. She recognized the voice on the phone, but she had to play it cool.

Once Karen hung up, she kept looking up different names and numbers online to see if she could locate the family. It took some time, but she located them.

Marcus picked up the phone, "Hello."

Karen spoke softly, "Ah yes, hello. My name is Karen Lotts. I am reaching out to you because I am aware of your situation with your family. You may find this a bit peculiar, but I am sure you find everything about what your daughters are going through peculiar. Lauren Pavlovsky is not an ordinary person, and she was brought up in an unorthodox situation. I am not calling to apologize for her behavior. I am simply calling to tell you to get out of town with your kids while you can."

Marcus looked at the phone. Then places the phone back to his ear.

She continues, "She is at my house and I will keep her here as long as I can. I bound the demon so that it can't hurt your children. If I can convince her to destroy it, I will. I just want you to leave town and never return. Can you do that?"

Marcus says, "Who are you? What in the world woman?"

Karen replies, "You don't have time for questions, and I can't explain everything. I made a mistake teaching her our ways. I am simply trying to fix what I created. Please get out of town while you can." and she hung up the phone.

Karen went down to the basement to work on a spell to keep the demon bound for a longer period of time. She kept working until the morning.

Lauren didn't realize that her nap turned into her sleeping until the next day. She came down for breakfast and her bags were packed. She decided to go back early since she figured out the connection with Charles.

She said, "Well I am packed to head back. I have to make it back to work this evening instead of tomorrow morning. It is a long drive."

She was shocked to see Karen working on something. She realized it had something to do with her.

She put her breakfast on the bookshelf and asked her "What are you doing?"

Karen admittedly replied, "I am working on an extended bonding incantation spell for Baymore. You seem to not care about these kids, so I am working on your soul and theirs. I didn't raise you to be working for the Devil."

Lauren laughed at her and walked towards the door.

Karen waved her hand and the door slammed closed.

Lauren said, "Oh wow, now you want to use your powers, very interesting. How long have you known?"

Karen replied, "I have been watching you and that little town on and off for a year now, but I didn't know it was this bad until you showed up. Experiments are one thing, but killing people is another thing. You are torturing little kids. These are innocent kids. I thought you were working on lost souls Lauren, not innocent children. When I saw kids dying in your ward, I knew something took a turn for the worse. Why are you choosing to go after children?"

Lauren shrugged her shoulders and said, "They are neither good nor evil, so it can go either way. Adults have already chosen their fate. It's too easy. You can't have fun with them. When I was little, I never got to choose. It was chosen for me. Why do they get to choose? How is that right? I want to prove that they don't."

Karen shook her head.

She waved her hand and opened the door.

She said, "Now you have a choice. You can either save that family and stay here with me or you can choose to make them suffer. I won't force you to stay."

Lauren said, "What do you mean force me to stay Karen? What do you know?"

Karen replied, "There are things in motion that you can't control. You either stay here and let them follow through or leave and suffer as they suffer. There will be several horrible deaths including your own my dear."

Lauren ran out of the basement not heeding Karen's warning. She took her luggage and went to her car. She drove back to her ward to find that Adeena was gone.

Chapter 13
Boomerang

A chair flies across the room.

"Adriel would you please hurry up and get in here. I don't know how much longer I can hold the door shut," yells Daniela.

She was gripping the door tightly. They were afraid that Adeena would come out of the room after them while Adriel was looking for something to hold her down with for the night. She seemed to be fine when they got home, but for some reason, she didn't want to be in the room alone.

Adriel finally came back, "Adeena, it's me Ads, I'm coming in, so don't throw anything, okay," he said trying to calm her down.

He slowly opened the door. She had a picture frame in her hand, but she saw it was him and she dropped it. He handed the rope off to his mother quickly so she couldn't see it.

He said confidently, "Don't worry. She isn't coming in unless you say it's okay. I'm closing the door and it's just going to be us for now?"

She nodded her head and he did exactly that.

He asked her, "What did they do to you in there?"

She shook her head and said, "Baymore showed me things, terrible things. I can't close my eyes Ads. I don't want to sleep anymore. I see them every time I go to sleep. I just can't, I can't."

Somehow, even through the gruesomeness of deformation, Adriel saw his sister still in there. He held onto her and he sat there wondering what she saw. She didn't tell him, but he knew it had to be something terrible for her not to want to go to sleep.

Adriel asked her why she kept attacking their parents.

She asked in a nasty way, "What are parents anyway?"

He pulled her off of him and said, "What do mean what are parents? Our mother and father? The people that raised us. They are standing right outside that door. They love us, Adeena."

She said, I don't have any parents, I just have you. You are all that matters to me. Those people out there are traitors. I don't want them near me or you. I will kill them if they touch me."

She pulled him back over to her and grabbed him tightly to make sure he didn't let go of her. He told her to stop.

She asked, "Don't you love me?"

He responded as calmly as he could, "Yes, but you're hurting me and I need to go right now. So, can you let go of me for a moment please?"

He tried not to sound scared of her at that moment. He knew if she heard any fear or nervousness in his tone, she wouldn't let him go.

She lifted her head very slowly with a smile on her face and said, "I guess I can try to learn to share but remember we are twins. We share a bond. My pain is yours."

She dug her nails into his arm until he bled. He jerked his arm away from her and stormed out of her room.

Adriel went to the bathroom to find some gauze and his mother followed him in. She saw what happened to his arm and helped him. She tried to be calm down and told him she heard what was going on.

He shook his head and said, "I don't think we will ever get her back."

Daniela said, "I have faith that anything is possible. Let's get your arm straight and get her tied down for the night."

He looked up at her and said, "You heard her, she can't sleep mother. This is going to be a rough night and you know it."

She sighed and said, "Well we will have to figure out a way to get her to sleep because there is no way she will be awake the whole night and cause havoc. We will have to take shifts staying out of her room, but we will have to get her to sleep."

Marcus came up the hallway and Daniela told him what happened. He went to get Daniela's medicine when she was sick that helped her sleep. They put some in Adeena's drink for Adriel to bring to her.

Adriel came into the room with a sandwich and drink. Arielle walked by the door with Peppa and Adeena threw her iPod out the door at the dog and it hit her in the ribs. The dog yelped and Adeena laughed. Adriel told her it wasn't necessary to behave that way. She shrugged it off and walked over to the chair by the window and sat down.

Adeena saw Adriel had food and told him she wasn't hungry. He told her it was just in case she became hungry.

She asked, "Who made it?"

Adriel responded to her that he did and that he knew if anyone else did, she wouldn't eat it.

He set it down on her dresser and said, "It's over here whenever you're ready to eat it. I will be in my room if you need me."

She stopped him and said, "I'm not going to apologize. I hope you know that. Since I can't let you see what I see, I want you to feel what I feel."

He said, "You've never been one to be sentimental." Then he walked out.

An hour had passed and a thud hit the floor. Daniela called Adriel to the room. He knocked on the door and there was no answer. He opened the door and he saw Adeena on the floor. He went over to check on her. He tapped on her shoulder, nudged her, and she didn't move. He told his mother to come and assist him in getting her to the bed. When Daniela went to get the ropes, Adeena started to mumble in her sleep. Adriel tried to listen to her, but he couldn't understand what she was saying.

At first, he thought it was gibberish, but he realized that she was speaking in another language. His mother came in and he told her to listen. Adeena flung her arm and smacked him in the face.

He said, "Okay let's just tie her down now."

She muttered out more words, but the last thing they heard was, "The light is so bright over you Adrienne."

Daniela stopped tying the knot. She looked at Adriel in disbelief and whispered, "No."

She leaned back over Adeena and finished tying the knot.

She said, "We have to tell your father."

Adriel didn't know what his mother was talking about. When they told Marcus he said, "The Peter's kid?"

Marcus put down the book he was reading and got up off the bed. He paced in the room and scratched his head.

Adriel asked, "Um can someone fill me in on what's going on please?"

Daniela turned to him and said, "Sorry son, okay. Catherine and Jordan's son was killed. He was obviously murdered by the demon that Dr. Pavlovsky was controlling. His name was Adrienne. Adeena said that the demon was showing her stuff, correct? So, I am thinking it was showing her the events of when the demon was killing people. I couldn't understand half of what she was muttering until she said his name."

Adriel thought to himself, it made so much sense why Adeena didn't want to sleep anymore. Why would anyone want to see anything like that? That would be horrifying. Adriel realized that they needed to wake her up.

He pulled his mother's arm and said, "We need to wake her up. This isn't right. We can't allow her to go through this."

She turned to Marcus and pleaded with him, "If we allow her to sleep, she will be tortured all night long."

He replied, "If she wakes up, she will fall asleep constantly regardless. That medicine is brutal. She doesn't have a choice."

Adriel felt so bad for her and his mother apologized to him. She told him to go watch out for her while they figured out what to do. Marcus would take the watch next and she would do the final so he could be there in the morning when she awakens.

The morning came and Adriel was in the room before she woke up. Arielle was with him so that Adeena could try to make peace with her. They had made her favorite breakfast for her. She woke up smelling eggs, strawberries on top of French toast with cream cheese, sausage, and orange juice. She smiled, but then she saw Arielle and started frowning.

She asked, "Why is the rug rat in my room?"

Adriel noticed that her hair was starting to turn back to its original color and she wasn't as pale as she was the night before.

Adriel replied, "Well if you want me to suffer, I want you to be nice to at least one other person in the house. Let's pick one. You can start with Arielle today and we can move on to mother and then father. Or you can choose them all and I can leave this little charade alone."

She growled and said, "Fine ugh, I will deal with mother and father, get her out of here."

Adriel turned and he took Arielle by the hand and walked out.

Adeena had to wait for him to return so that she could eat since she was still tied up. When he returned, he had their mother with him this time. She saw her come into the room and she growled again.

Adriel put up his hand and said, "Tisk, tisk, now you said you would allow her in. You can't have your breakfast until you behave with our mother in here. Do you agree Adeena? Can I trust you to not hurt or be nasty with her?"

She looked at her food and replied, "Yes yes, fine. Now untie me so I can freaking eat. Gosh, I am hungry."

He walked over to her and untied her legs and sat her up.

He then went to her right arm and said, "I am only doing one arm, and I will be in the chair watching you. Behave and eat your food. Our mom will be making conversation with you and you better be nice the whole time."

Adriel placed the tray on her lap and she ate her food ignoring her mom.

Daniela turned the TV on and said, "What would you like to watch?"

Adeena shrugged her shoulders and said, "Put cartoons on. I didn't get to watch any of that while I was locked up."

Daniela turned it to cartoons and she noticed that Adeena was stuffing her face and not taking a break in between chewing. She told her to slow down. Adeena ignored her. Daniela got up and stepped over to her. Adeena growled at her.

Adriel heard her and said, "No, take a step back."

Daniela told Adriel to stay in his place, but she forgot that Adeena wasn't herself. She turned back around and saw that Adeena had the fork in her hand ready to stab her. Daniela stopped in her tracks and sat back down. Adeena went back to eating again.

Daniela looked back over at Adriel, nodded her head, and mouthed sorry. Daniela asked Adeena how she slept.

Adeena laughed and said, "How do you think I slept mother, dear."

She flung her tied-up arm in the air.

She said, "I had horrifying nightmares and I'm tied to a bed. Would you like to try it?"

She lunged at her with a smirk on her face while she laughed hysterically. The tray fell on the floor with a clang.

Daniela got up and walked to the door. Adriel got up and picked up the tray. He tied her arm back to the bedpost and told her he would be back. He knew that he was reaching for a connection, but it's going to take some time.

As Adriel got downstairs with the tray to clean up the mess, Charles came knocking on the door. He looked as if he had been hit with a boomerang. Adriel asked him what was wrong. Charles made a glass of water from the sink and he drank all of it in one gulp. Charles ran from his house to Adriel's without stopping. His stepmother had taken him to town that morning to stop by the store. They had gotten groceries for dinner and he went to the doctor's office to look for the box and it wasn't there.

"What," screamed Adriel.

His father came into the kitchen to see why Adriel was yelling.

Charles explained to Marcus what he told Adriel and he became frantic.

Another knock was at the door. Marcus looked over at Adriel and Charles. They both shrugged their shoulders. Marcus told Adriel to run upstairs and keep Adeena quiet. Charles stood behind the wall in the kitchen listening to who was at the door. It was Sindy. She told them she was taking an extra shift today to make sure no one was checking on Adeena's. She wanted to see how she was doing and to let them know that the doctor would be back on duty the next day around three that afternoon. She also would be leaving the night. She wanted to make sure she told them. She would get in touch with them after she found somewhere to live. Marcus thanked her and that she should head to town and be safe.

Charles came from behind the wall and asked him if she seemed fine? Marcus shrugged his shoulders and went to talk to his wife.

Charles went to knock on Adeena's door and opened it. Adeena smiled at Charles and said, "Well hello there, come in."

Adriel was shocked to see her smile without being rude for once. He didn't know why she was doing it, but it was strange. Charles ignored it and was not alarmed by her actions. He told Adriel what happened but Adriel didn't seem to care. He was still trying to figure out what to do about the demon.

Adeena watched Charles with admiration.

Charles said to Adriel, "You know we still have to figure a way to get those bones and Dr. Pavlovksy's blood. We need to check out her house. I know where she lives. I'll try to go there and see where everything is."

Adeena interrupted with enthusiasm and said, "I don't mind helping you. You seem to know what you're talking about and have this macho attitude about you, which is awesome. I can sense that you want to help us get this fixed. If you guys don't mind, I would like to do my part."

She winked at Charles, but she saw Adriel's face looking disgusted. She immediately changed her attitude.

She said, "Well I mean if Ads don't mind me helping."

Charles turned around and became annoyed.

He said, "I don't care, as long as we can kill this thing, I'm good."

Adriel had no idea what Adeena had up her sleeve, but he knew Charles didn't care about what she was saying. He had planned on killing Baymore. Adeena seemed to want to get out of the house and away from their family. He also knew something was up with Adeena and she wasn't acting like her normal self. He had to figure out what she was up to. So, he told her that she had to stay behind until she could be trusted.

As the day went on Marcus received a call from a strange woman telling him to leave town. He didn't know who she was. He went to Daniela and told her about this strange and unusual call.

He said, "This woman named Karen Lotts called me and said that Lauren Pavlovsky is staying with her. She knew that we had gotten Adeena out of the ward. She wasn't going to tell Dr. Pavlovsky about it, but that as long as we get our family out of town and away from here that we would be safe. She also said that she had bound the demon as best she could. She will try to convince the doctor to put the demon away or kill it. I'm not sure what she meant by that, but she asked me to leave town immediately. She wouldn't explain to me how she knew all of this. I think Sindy told her. Why would Sindy just show up this morning and then say she was leaving town like that. It is oddly strange for all of this to happen out of nowhere."

Daniela was frustrated that he had interrupted her soap opera. She barely heard everything he said.

She said, "Honey, wait, who called and how did she get our number? You think Sindy gave her all of this information and Dr. Pavlovsky was at her house. Was she holding her hostage or something? Wait, what? I am totally lost."

He said, "This woman called us out of the blue and told me all of this. She never gave me any information on who told her this information. She just said that we needed to leave town. She tried to help us and she would keep the doctor at her place as long as she could. I think we should listen to her."

Daniela gave her husband the worst possible look and led him out of the room. They went straight to Adeena's room and she opened the door. Adriel, Charles, and Adeena turned and looked at them.

Daniela said, "You think right now is the best time to flee? Look at her. She doesn't even trust us. She hates us. She can't even sit in a room with her mother and have a civil conversation and you want to flee. Yeah Marcus, let's leave with this suicidal mission right now and die."

She stormed off leaving him standing in the doorway while the children watched him.

He apologized to the three of them and closed the door.

Charles looked over at Adriel and said, "I told you, dude, I got this."

Adriel knew that the boomerang from earlier had come back around. It had hit him in the pit of his stomach. He just looked at Charles and all he could think about was Charles killing one of his sisters.

Adriel said, "There's gotta be another way."

Chapter 14
Serene in Disguise

Arielle woke up and came into the room with Peppa and saw her sister asleep. She walked over to wake Adriel up to tell him that she was hungry and that their parents were still in bed. He told her that she shouldn't be in there. He let her know he would be down in a few to fix breakfast and to go watch TV. She started to walk out of the room but then Adeena woke up.

She didn't yell or scream this time, she just looked over at her and said, "Good morning Arielle. Did you sleep well last night? I know I didn't."

Adeena smiled at her as she walked out of the room. Peppa growled low looking back at Adeena as they left the room.

Adriel asked her, "Why do you hate her so much? She is your sister."

Adeena replied, "Why do you love her more than me? I should come first, not that little rodent. I have to go to the bathroom. Can you at least release me so I can use the bathroom?"

He was startled by her answer. He walked over to untie her, but as he did, he thought about when he was in the bathroom with Arielle. Adeena had previously told him something about her jealousy with their sister, so he stopped.

He said, "You know I love you both the same. I will do for you just as I do for her. You are both my sisters. She is just smaller and that is why she gets the hugs and attention. You and I have been together longer and you don't need that attention from me. Well, at least I thought you didn't. If that is why you have been acting out, I'm so sorry."

He untied her and let her go to the bathroom. Adriel stood on the outside of the bathroom thinking of all the times she would push Arielle around trying to hurt her. He never once realized that it was because of him.

While Adeena was in the bathroom, she began crying. She thought he loved Arielle more than her. She never knew that he was just treating her special because she was little. She thought about them growing up playing and fighting other people. How he would defend her because people would make fun of her hairstyles, or the way she would dress. He was always there for her and now he was doing the same for Arielle. She didn't think that she was taking away from him helping her. She washed her hands and opened the door.

As Adeena came out of the bathroom, her mother walked by and somehow, she became angry again. One of the visions from her dream enters her mind. She saw a mother banging the daughter's head on the floor until the child was unconscious. Adeena attacked her mother and slammed her into the wall.

Adriel called for his father while he tried to pull Adeena off of their mother, but she was so strong. He didn't know what was going on, but for some reason, Adeena was grabbing her mother's head and was pounding it into the wall.

Daniela was trying to put her arms in between her to push her off. She was starting to lose consciousness. It took both Adriel and Marcus to get Adeena off of her. Daniela fell to the floor while Adeena was screaming and yelling.

Marcus and Adriel took Adeena back to her room and tied her back to the bed.

Marcus asked Adriel, "What happened?"

Adriel responded, "I don't know. She was in the bathroom and when she opened the door she came out and attacked her. I don't know why."

Marcus turned to Adeena and yelled at her, "Why did you attack her?"

She laughed and said, "You are traitors. Both of you." And she spits at him.

Marcus balled his fist up and Adriel grabbed his arm and yelled "No!"

Marcus walked out to the room.

Adriel asked Adeena what she meant by them being traitors.

She said, "Every night I dream of everything that demon has done and had made others do. Some of the people are killing and some are tortured. I can't actually see the person, but I know someone was killing them. Baymore wants me to suffer and I know if our parents had never sent me to that woman I would never have been put in this situation. I keep seeing parents killing their kids and I feel them dying. Apart of me feels like I am dying with them. I hate Marcus and Daniela. This is their fault."

Adriel knew it was what Baymore wanted her to think.

He said with as much convincing as he could, "Adeena, that demon came to you when you were a little child before any of this started to put anger and jealousy in your heart. When Arielle was born, you started on this course then. Baymore knew then, that you would be like this. Dr. Pavlovsky is the one to blame, not our parents. They didn't know that she was doing this. If you need someone to be mad at or blame, blame Dr. Pavlovsky and that demon. We saved you from that institution, we may not know how to get the images out of your head, but we can get rid of the demon."

Adriel got up, went to his father, and told him that they needed to talk.

Adriel told his father what he thought Charles was going to do. He felt that Charles had planned on killing one of his sisters. The spell required someone close to the one that he loved to die for the demon to be banished. He also informed his father that he wanted to be sacrificed instead. He knew that Dr. Pavlovsky was targeting the entire family and to save the family, he needed to sacrifice himself to save the family. He felt that once it was done Adeena's mind would be better and Arielle would be safe. They could leave and Dr. Pavlovsky wouldn't be after them anymore.

His father yelled at him and told him about the phone call. Then the call he received from Sindy late yesterday evening as well. Marcus didn't understand quite what was going on. He and his mother were under the impression that someone was looking out for them. Maybe they needed to come up with another plan to get out of town and maybe the demon wouldn't follow.

Adriel was somewhat pleased to hear all of this, but he still didn't think it was going to save them. He knew that once the demon had a hold of your soul, it would always find you. His father didn't believe him because Karen told them to get out of town. He told Adriel that they were going to start packing and they were moving back to his hometown in Texas. He had already called his parents and told them that they were coming.

Adriel wasn't happy about moving and he left the room. He knew his father and mother left Texas was to get away from there. The only reason they would go back is because of the demon. He knew that his mother wouldn't agree to this unless she had to. He went back to Adeena's room and sat on the end of her bed.

She asked, "Did you tell them about what I said?"

He said, "No I didn't get a chance. We are moving to Texas to Papa's tomorrow. We won't be able to have time to kill Baymore."

"What do you mean? We need to get rid of the demon Ad," she said panicking.

She started pulling at her ropes trying to get free. He just sat there feeling miserable. He ignored that she was jerking at the ropes. She almost got loose when their father came in because he heard the noise. He went over and slammed her arm back on the bed. He yelled for Adriel to snap out of it and help him.

Later that day, Charles came over and had informed Adriel of some good news. He told Adriel that his father would be going to town by the auto body shop to get some parts. He asked Adriel if he wanted to go with him. Adriel knew this would be a great opening for him to get the things they needed. Even though they were on different pages of how to kill the demon, Adriel felt they could at least try it his way before they left town.

So, he told his father that he wanted to go with Charles this last time before they left tomorrow. Marcus agreed and told him not to spend all day. Before he left, he pulled his father aside and told him about what Adeena disclosed to him. He realized that even though he was about to do something drastic he may never see his parents ever again. He thought they needed to know what she was dealing with. When he divulged the information about her dreams and her visions, his father was very concerned. He told Adriel to go on and make sure he didn't get into any trouble. Adriel knew his father was in deep thought.

As they approached the hardware store, Charles asked his father if they could be dropped off at the convenience store so they could get some snacks and sodas. They told him they would catch up with him later at the park. He agreed and he drove off. The doctor lived two streets down from the store. They walked over and her car wasn't there. It was around two-thirty in the afternoon and Sindy had already told Charles that she was at the institution.

Charles told Adriel to stay outside to keep watch. The upstairs window was open. Charles hopped on the patio and climbed up the drainpipe to get to the second floor. Adriel was in awe that he could do it without a problem. Instead of watching his surroundings, he was watching Charles climb in the window.

Once Charles was in the window, Adriel started looking around. He noticed there was a tree in her backyard where the ground had been broken. Adriel walked over and started digging with his hands. He uncovered a small tin box. When he opened it, there was a bone, a valve of blood, and a piece of torn cloth inside just like at the office. He closed it and took the tin back over to the house. He called up to Charles and told him to come back out.

Charles came to the window with a smile on his face and said, "Jackpot" holding up another tin box.

Adriel was ecstatic.

Charles made his way down, but this time he slid down from the second-floor roof and jumped onto the patio.

Adriel showed him the box he found and Charles raised his up and clanged it to Adriel's as if they had wine glasses.

Charles said, "Let's get out of here, partner."

They put the boxes in a sack then ran down the street to the convenience store. They got snacks and sodas from the store and went to sit at the park to wait for Charles's dad.

As they waited, Charles told Adriel that he had everything planned out perfectly. Adriel was feeling great until he had said that. He placed his chips down and stopped him.

He said, "My parents are making us move tomorrow. If we are going to do this, we have to do it tonight."

"Wait, what?" Charles said.

Adriel replied, "Yes, they don't think killing the demon will do anything and they don't think we have enough time. They think Dr. Pavlovsky is still out of town at some woman's house. If we are going to do this, we need to do it tonight."

Charles took a bite of his sandwich and said, "Meet me at the creek around ten tonight. We will end this."

Back at home, Adeena was trying her hardest to be nice to her parents. She promised Adriel while he was gone, she would not harm them or give them a hard time. Adeena knew that her visions had nothing to do with her parents and she knew they weren't the ones doing it, but she had a hard time separating her visions from reality. When her mother would bring her lunch, she had to announce herself before entering the room. Adeena knew that she had to remain calm and close her eyes. That was the only way that her mother would be able to enter the room without being harmed.

Unfortunately, Adeena wouldn't let Marcus come into the room at all. By the time Adriel returned, it was dinner time and his father told him that she didn't do anything wrong and things seemed fine. He asked him if he enjoyed his time with Charles. He wanted to know if Charles was going to leave like they were? Adriel nodded his head and went upstairs to Adeena to tell her what happened.

He noticed that the majority of her clothes had been packed and she seemed to be in a good mood. She asked if she could join them for dinner that night.

He said, "Well how about you sit over there in the chair for dinner this evening. Arielle and I will join you?"

She replied, "That would be great."

Dinner time came and Arielle came with Peppa. Adeena was in her chair by the window beside Adriel. She wasn't tied up and the plate setting was already done. Arielle was happy to see her smiling. Adeena told her it was okay and

Peppa ran over and lay beside her. Daniela was outside the door listening and she looked over to Marcus and gave him a thumbs up.

As dinner was ending, Adriel felt a chill come in the air. The phone rang and they could hear their father talking. He became louder, but Adriel couldn't make out what he said. A gust of wind came out of nowhere, but the window wasn't open. A shadow had formed over the top of the children. Marcus threw open the door. He saw Adeena being thrown out of her chair and into the wall behind Peppa. Arielle was picked up and was hovering over the top of them. Adriel tried to get to her but he was blocked by a forcefield. Adeena balled up in the corner of the room. Daniela ran to Adeena to shield her, but his time she didn't reject her mother.

Baymore wouldn't let go of Arielle. Arielle screamed and cried. Marcus and Adriel were trying their hardest to get to Arielle, but the more they tried the more the forcefield broadened around her. Adriel realized that his father had brought the phone into the room with him, but he had thrown it on the bed.

He went to the phone and said, "Hello?"

The woman on the other end said, "Adriel, I know you don't know me, but I need you to place me on speaker, please. I can help you."

Adriel didn't hesitate, he immediately hit the speaker button and the woman started speaking in German. While she was speaking, Adeena and Arielle saw Baymore getting angry. As he got angrier, the forcefield got smaller. Adriel knew the woman was casting a spell of some kind. He wanted to drop the phone so he could get closer, but he knew he couldn't. There was a loud horrible roar from the demon. A huge gust of wind pushed Adriel back. Daniel turned away and she covered Adeena's face.

Marcus saw Arielle drop and caught her. Adriel knew that meant that Baymore was gone. Adeena pushed her mother away from her and she ran to Adriel.

The woman on the phone said, "Adriel, my name is Karen Lotts. I am Dr. Pavlovksy's great aunt. She is back in town. I have bound the demon again, but only for a short time. I can't keep it bound forever. You have to kill it or put him back into Hell. Lauren will not do it. She wants to keep him under her control. She doesn't understand that this demon only wants souls. It doesn't care about her or what she wants. It will kill her to get what it wants. Please do this soon or your family will die."

Then she hung up.

Adriel turned to father and said, "Do you believe me now? I have to do this."

Adriel looked down at both his sisters and told them he loved them and he walked out to his room.

Chapter 15
Purgatory

Adeena felt like she was stuck in a place that she couldn't get out of. She knew she didn't put herself there and she screamed for help, but no one could hear her.

"Where am I?" Adeena said to herself.

A split second between each dream was all she got, "Well" she thought.

A dream felt like a lifetime. Adeena called her dreams Purgatory. It was a place between Hell and Real Life for her. While she was awake, she felt tortured by her parents. She didn't know the names of the people that were killing and hurting the kids, but she could tell that they were the parents. When she was looking at her father, she wanted to kill him. The man that hurt the little girl in her dream looked exactly like her father. The girl looked just like Adeena, but her hair was different and she had freckles. She wasn't sure why that one made her so angry. Every time she saw her father the vision appeared. She wanted to tell her mother about it, but she thought she would get mad at her. Purgatory was the worst feeling and she knew she had to sleep or she would become someone else if she didn't sleep.

Meanwhile, Adriel looked over at the clock and it was nine forty-eight. He knew it was too early to head to the creek. Charles hadn't come to the house to get his sisters so he was curious to find out what he was up to. He went to

Adeena's room and asked her to go out to the woods with him.

Adeena was reprieved that he came to save him from her dreadful night. She didn't want to take the sleeping pills. She saw the concern in her brother's eyes.

Adeena asked, "Are you sure you want me to go with you?"

Adriel was hesitant to answer her question because he didn't know if Charles would try to kill her. If that would've been the case, he would've already come and got her.

He said, "Yes, I need someone brave to go with me just in case Charles does something stupid and we mess up."

She jumped up out of her bed, put her boots on, and they quietly went out the back door while their parents were asleep. Adriel took a huge gamble on bringing her and he knew it, but he also knew that Charles didn't know what he had planned.

Adriel walked to their favorite spot by the creek and he didn't see Charles there. He noticed that there was already a hole dug up. It wasn't a huge hole. It was small enough for a child. He wasn't sure what Charles had planned. He opened his phone and noticed it said nine fifty-six.

Adeena looked over at Adriel and asked him, "So, what is Charles's plan by the way?"

Adriel could feel his stomach drop. He didn't want to tell her what he thought, but he responded by saying, "I honestly don't know. All he keeps saying is he has this."

Adriel's eyes were wide open searching for Charles since the only thing that lit the area was the moon, he had a hard time seeing things. Even with the moon, it was difficult to see the trees that covered the area.

Charles still hadn't come and Adeena was curious as to why she was tagging along. So, she started to walk around. She wandered off and she stumbled upon the tree that had the marking with the "X" on it. She then saw the rest of the message under it.

She stepped back and yelled, "Are you freaking serious Ads? Am I bait or something?"

Adriel was confused by what she said because just then he saw Charles walking up. He was pulling something behind him.

He didn't look over at her, but he responded, "What are you yelling about over there? No one is baiting anyone. Stop being paranoid. Charles, what took you so long?"

Adriel started walking towards him. He noticed that he was pulling something behind him and it was making a loud squeaking sound. He couldn't see what he was pulling. Adriel stopped in his tracks when he saw Arielle's red wagon. Something was lying off the end of it.

Adriel yells, "Charles, why do you have Arielle's wagon?"

Charles didn't respond and Adeena fell to the ground crying and yelling out no several times. As Charles finally approached, he was out of breath and Adriel placed his hand on Charles's chest telling him to stop.

Adriel says, "You can't do this. This isn't right."

Charles smacks his hand away and said, "I love her too man, but if we don't do this. It will never end."

Adriel became angry and said, "She's my sister. What do you mean you love her too?"

Charles shook his head and walked over to the hole he had dug up earlier that day and put the bones from both boxes. He ignored what Adriel said. He then went back over to the wagon and started to pick up the bag with a body in it. Adriel pushed him and he fell with the body.

Charles got up abruptly and approached him.

He said, "Look, if we don't do this, that demon will win and both of our families will die, not just yours."

Neither of them realized at this moment that Baymore was hovering over top of them as they were arguing. The sky got completely dark as the moon had been covered.

Adeena yelled out, "Look up!"

She balled up in a knot on the ground by a tree.

They both slowly looked up and Baymore was piercing down over the top of them. Suddenly, knives appeared in their hands and the demon had them pointing them at each other. Adeena was crying and screaming at them to stop. Adriel was amazed that he could actually see Baymore this time.

Adriel had seen something glowing in the distance from the corner of his eyes. He turned his head and he saw this glowing blue florescent light behind Charles in the distance and didn't know what was going on. He began to fight with all his strength against the force that pushed him to place the knife into his best friend's chest. Adriel kept looking past Charles and saw that the glow turned into this boy as it approached.

The boy grabbed his hand and told Adriel, "You know what you have to say. I gave you my light. Use what was given to you and you will survive anything."

A surge of energy entered Adriel's body. The boy turned around and disappeared into the light. The words came to Adriel as he remembered it, "I love the light and the light is mine." Baymore became infuriated, but he had no choice but to release him. Adriel took the knife out of Charles' hand and threw it on the bag.

Baymore reached over and grabbed Adeena by her throat. As he did so, Charles picked the knife back up and leaned over to cut her arm with his knife. Then he ran to Adriel and did the same. He knew he couldn't complete the ritual without the blood of his loved ones. Baymore saw what he did. The demon released Adeena. Charles took the bag and he put the body in the hole.

Adriel turned around and yelled, "No!"

Adriel and Adeena ran over to see who it was. They saw it wasn't Arielle, it was Sasha. Charles had sedated her somehow. Charles opened several valves and poured the blood on Sasha along with the cloth from the tin boxes. He then took his knife in his hand. He cut his hand, then stabbed her in her heart.

Adeena yelled, "No Charles Stop!"

Adriel looked at his sister fell to her knees and cried. He realized that he had seen this before. His dream flashed before his eyes. He looked back at Charles and he began quietly crying.

The boy reappeared in the distance and watched him. Adriel felt a sense of calm when he saw the boy this time. Adriel knew that this had to happen for everything to end. It started to rain heavily and Charles was still stabbing her. The blood was hitting Adeena in her face. Baymore let out thunderous laughter as he began to disappear.

Adriel calmly went over and took the knife out of Charles's hand. He tossed the knife in the wagon. He then took a shovel and started to fill the hole. Adriel wanted to forget what just happened, but he knew he couldn't escape what he saw.

He couldn't understand why Charles couldn't stop stabbing her as he did or how could someone like that love her too? He just knew that was a brutal and cold way for her to die.

As soon as Adriel finished covering up the body, Charles placed three big stones on the end of the grave and he kissed them. Adeena stopped crying and was confused. Adriel was also confused by his action. They glanced at each other in shock. Adriel thought to himself maybe he did love her. They walked out of the woods without speaking a word until they got to the road and then the rain stopped.

Charles told Adriel he will be catching a ride with Sindy to Chicago in the morning before the sun rises and that he will miss them all. He was sorry if he hurt them in any way. He made sure that Sasha didn't feel anything. He asked Sindy for the medicine to sedate her so she wouldn't know what happen. Sindy didn't know why he needed it, but she agreed to help. He loved them and that he will never forget the friendship and will cherish them all.

Charles handed the wagon over to Adriel and told him goodbye. He got on his bike and rode in the opposite direction from his house. Adeena and Adriel watched him as he rode off.

Adeena turned to Adriel and said, "I don't know what to think."

Adriel didn't respond to her, he just turned to head back to the house.

The next morning, as they were packing the vehicles to leave, the Sheriff came to their house to inform them that Charles and Sasha were missing. Also, Dr. Pavlovsky was brutally stabbed in her house. They couldn't find where someone had broken in, but they didn't see any disturbances in the house. They didn't know if there was a connection, but between the kids missing and the brutal murders, they would like to know why they were moving so soon.

Marcus informed them that they had papers to release their daughter and he felt better raising their kids closer to family. He was sorry for what was going on, but it had nothing to do with them.

Adriel didn't remember them getting any paperwork. Somehow Sindy must have done something before she left to get that done. His father showed the Sheriff something to convince him otherwise.

The Sheriff handed the papers back and wanted to make sure that he kept his phone number the same and to give him the forwarding address so that they keep him updated on the investigation.

Marcus asked if they were suspects. The Sheriff told him no, just thought that since she was released a day before the death, it was suspicious.

Marcus said, "Well Sheriff, if we are not suspects, then we don't have to give you any information or participate in your investigation. Now we will be on our way. I hope this investigation goes well."

The Sheriff huffed, stumped back to his car, and drove off. Marcus waited for him to get down the street and told everyone to jump in.

When they got in the truck, Marcus asked Adriel, "Ads what was that all about? I know you know what's going on."

Adriel responded, "You wouldn't believe me if I told you."

He looked out the window and turned his iPod on. Marcus looked back at Adeena, she seemed to be fine, but Adeena was still struggling in her mind. She never told Adriel that the visions were still there and the voices were still there. Baymore may be gone, but everything is still roaming around. She felt it was her fight. She was going to take it one day at a time for him. She plugged up the iPod and turned the music up to block out the sounds of what she believed to be purgatory. Her brother sacrificed more than enough. As she looks out the window traveling towards an adventure for her new life, she realizes it's her turn to fight her demons.

About the Author

S.M. Robinson, the author of *Neither Good nor Evil*, hails from Virginia with her family their whole lives. She enjoys playing board, card, and video games with her family. Some of her inspirations come from movies and books like Shadow Hunters, The Hobbit, Lord of the Rings as well as Crime Investigative Shows. She enjoys watching movies that have climaxes and twists to keep you on the edge of your seat. She hopes her books will do the same for her readers. When she is not spending time with her family, she is writing. Now with the first book of the trilogy, Neither Good nor Evil has been completed, she is beyond excited for her trilogy to come alive for the world to see.